Maggie Brooks was born in 1954 and studied at the National Film School. Her work includes a feature film and a TV play for Oscar-winning producer David Puttnam, a number of short films, and a TV play, *Balance of Nature*, which was shown with great success in the summer of 1983. *Loose Connections* was also turned into a successful film.

Maggie Brooks lives in London.

Loose Connections

MAGGIE BROOKS

AN ABACUS BOOK

First published in Great Britain by Chatto & Windus: The Hogarth
Press in 1984

Published by Futura Publications, a Division of Macdonald & Co
(Publishers) Ltd in 1985
Published in Abacus by Sphere Books in 1990

Reproduced, printed and bound in Great Britain by
The Guernsey Press Co. Ltd, Guernsey, Channel Islands.

ISBN 0 349 10138 8

Sphere Books Ltd
A Division of
Macdonald and Co. (Publishers) Ltd,
Orbit House, 1 New Fetter Lane, London EC4A 1AR

A member of Maxwell Macmillan Pergamon Publishing Corporation

For Elsie E. E. Brooks

Chapter 1

They drove out to Cookham one Sunday to inspect the parts they planned to order. They had decided to build a kit car and were torn between a blueprint based on Escort parts and another which used a Mini sub-frame.

They sauntered into the shop with the idea of sounding out the salesman on the relative merits of each. The salesman eyed them dubiously. They were three, in truth, rather dizzy-looking girls.

'Well, I could show you the parts but I don't suppose they'd mean much to you. Is he not coming in himself?'

There was a moment's pause in which Kay studied the Unipart calendar. A girl clutching a giant spark plug between oiled breasts.

'Who?' asked Sally frostily. She held his gaze steadily. He broke first and rubbed the bald spot on his head.

'Ah,' he said evenly, 'I get you. So you're er going to have a go yourself, are you? Well, walk this way . . .' He lifted the hatch and allowed them through. 'You'll have to mind your clothes, it's not very tidy.' They trailed behind him through the banks of spares that were pigeonholed up to the ceiling. 'Don't get many young ladies in here,' he confided affably to Laurie. 'I'll tell you though. It can be an expensive mistake if you don't know what you're doing. It's not like Lego.'

They ended up the excursion in his seedy bolt-hole at the back. It smelt like a fox had been through it, an aggressive mixture of sweat and tobacco. 'If you don't mind me giving you some advice,' he was saying as he riffled through the stack of pamphlets, 'I mean, if you're quite serious, I'd suggest this little . . .' he held it up triumphantly, 'thing here. The Scallywag.' It was painted red and yellow, was slightly rounded at both ends and looked like the car used by Noddy and Big Ears. 'Just the right size for shopping in traffic. Popular with the ladies. You know, antique dealers and that.' He ran his eye over the pamphlet. 'Simple enough for a child to assemble. Under guidance of course. Actually I did hear the local cubs are doing one as a project.'

'You misunderstand,' said Laurie gently. 'We want to build something functional and solid. The Cherokee looks far more suitable. Something in that style.'

'And quite roomy,' said Kay.

'Yes,' said Laurie, 'it may have to go up the Himalayas and we can't afford the Sherpas.'

His eyes roamed over the three women. None of them smiled. They were still in dispute over where the jeep was going, but it was early days.

The parts duly arrived at the mews garage. The blueprint was deficient in lots of vital information and the instructions took for granted certain basic grounding which they did not have.

But they *did* have Laurie. She was small and elfin and looked about fourteen, but she was extraordinarily capable. She mended stereos, took apart televisions, knew everything there was to know about roof-lagging, could fix gas installations. She taught arc-welding in a metal workshop. If there was anything she couldn't tackle successfully, they had yet to see it.

So, under guidance, they took everything step by step, approaching each job as a separate challenge. Eventually, they came to function as an intuitive unit, communicating against the shattering din of the welding by minimal signals.

As the jeep took shape, they settled on the Women's Event in Munich as a fitting first trip. The Himalayas was too far, and Kay's husband would never let her go. Laurie was outvoted because she couldn't drive and so wasn't entitled to an equal say, although this was not entirely fair since her test was coming up and there wasn't any doubt she'd pass.

Kay's husband came on a state visit and was rather taken aback. He hadn't really taken it seriously till now. The body of the jeep had a toy-like quality, but there was no doubt it *was* a jeep, a serious substantial fact, and there was no way just by peering under the sills that one could tell it had been made by women. He didn't say much but they felt he was impressed by their commitment, at least.

The day when the engine first turned over was one of great elation. Champagne tickertaped across the windscreen and the three of them got drunk, more on their own achievement than the alcohol. It was a heady feeling. Kay and Sally walked round in a glow for several days, feeling that people in the street could see that they'd just done something wonderful.

They got maps and started planning their route along the Rhine.

They never did find out how the local paper got hold of it. There was a call. They didn't actually think about it too hard. 'It'll be crass,' Laurie warned, but she offered no real objection. It seemed positive to have a write-up just because other women might be interested. That was all. They forgot about it until, one Saturday, the reporter arrived with a photographer.

'So this was by way of being a personal challenge, was it?' he asked, circling the car with a blank and jaundiced eye – giant sunflowers, lost dogs, miniature majorettes, it was all the same. The photographer knelt to frame a better picture up their nostrils.

'It was just something we wanted to do,' said Sally crisply, with an eye to avoiding his feed lines. 'So we did it.'

'Did any of your friends: people generally, find it strange, girls wanting to build cars?' He raised one quizzical but basically uninterested eyebrow. What inspired you to build this fine model of Brighton Pavilion out of fishbones?

Sally and Laurie exchanged glances. Kay, who'd been brought up to fill awkward silences and make people feel at ease, helpfully volunteered Keith's views. 'Well, my husband weren't too keen on me coming home covered in oil . . . but now . . . well, he thinks it's very competent . . . he *was* surprised . . .' She was going to say, 'that it passed the M.O.T.', but Laurie cut across her sharply, noticing his shorthand suddenly oscillating across the notepad.

'*We* weren't surprised at all,' she said firmly. 'Any incompetence that women show with machinery's just been socialised into them by men.'

'Oh yeah?' he said, with weary insolence. Just what he needed, a rabid, humourless feminist giving him an earful.

'Yeah.' She stuck her chin up at him, sneering.

Shame really, he thought. A bit of a waste. She had rather a good body.

'Right, line 'em up, Wally,' he said, snapping his book closed.

The photographer waved his arms as though herding sheep.

'This way, ladies please,' and the thing was happening so fast that they had no time to protest before they were posed before the radiator grille, glowering. Wally's eye appeared from over the viewfinder, apologetically. 'You couldn't undo that top button a bit, the blonde on the right . . .' He looked at Sally. She withered him with her stare and the shutter clicked on the uncompromising hostility of three humourless, proselytising dykes.

The article was no better than they expected.

'At least we don't look like cheesecakes,' said Kay, trying to scratch for any little crumb of comfort.

'No, we look like plainclothes prison warders,' said Sally.

The text ascribed to them the twittering inconsequentiality of breathless schoolgirls and the photo made them look like muscle-bound women piledrivers from a Soviet propaganda poster.

The headline read: YOU CAN TINKER WITH OUR GASKETS ANY DAY.

Sally wondered vaguely if it had taken long to compose, and what sort of mind had composed it. And whether he was safe on the streets.

As they walked away from the newsagents Laurie read it out loud.

' "My husband was impressed," said attractive Kay Whiting, thirty-two of Trellick Tower. The enterprising threesome dug out books from the local library and pestered local motor spares dealers . . .' Kay squealed, groaned, went into a convulsion, seized the paper and stuffed it forcefully into a passing bin.

Although she laughed about it, Sally found it difficult to put the article out of her mind. It spoke too loudly of the casual contempt men had for women. It wasn't nice to be seen as three funny pet dogs, trying to stand on their hind legs. She sat at her desk staring at the manuscript she was typing. It was a collection of quotes and newspaper clippings that she'd been putting together for some time. They were linked together with her own thoughts and comments. She had an idea that collating disparate but connected ideas in this way would give her a clearer picture of the world, and that it was a worthwhile use of the long summer break from the school, to set her thoughts in order. She was doing it for herself as much as for anyone else. But the conference and the trip were assuming more and more importance as the paperwork grew, and she had a feeling somehow that Munich could be a watershed in her life. Now that the jeep was finished, she found the time dragged, and she was yearning to get away from London.

Kay, preparing the dinner, was also thinking about the trip. She was wondering when would be the best time to mention it. Keith *was* very good, she told herself dutifully. He bathed Benjamin sometimes, he often put him to bed. He helped around the house. But each time he completed some self-appointed task he always felt the need to announce it: 'Got a good shine on that kitchen floor,' or 'Well, that's another lot of washing-up out of the way.' Kay was grateful. She rewarded him on the same carrot-and-stick system she used with Benji. But sometimes as she ritually mouthed, 'What a lovely surprise, everything scrubbed and put away,' she found herself mentally adding, Who's a good boy then? I've only done that twenty times this week. She sometimes felt as though she had the care of two infants, not one.

Lately, she had got out of the habit of praising the room vacuumed or the shopping fetched. Praising him presupposed the chores to be her own natural lot. Since she also had a working job, she couldn't see it. Once his reward dwindled to little more than an approving sniff Keith had lost any incentive to battle with the eternal round that made the household function. And then, what with her spending two or three nights a week at the workshop, she sensed that he was beginning to feel hard done by.

She thought she might leave asking him for a few days. It had to be broached in the right way. Perhaps she could ask Laurie and Sally not to mention the trip. There again, she didn't want them to think Keith was any problem in case it prejudiced them against him. It was already a rather delicate juggling act.

Laurie and Sally thought of him as a decent bloke but relations with him were somewhere between strained and non-existent. Laurie's theory was that he was shy and she often asked him questions about technical things and tried to make him recognise she respected his advice. Sally had a different theory. He answered pleasantries in a polite, perfunctory way and always avoided eye contact. 'I don't think he likes us.'

Laurie was quite sure she'd made some progress. 'Oh, course he does,' she said. 'He's just diffident with women. You have to draw him out a bit.'

'Hello, Keith. How's the plastering?' asked Laurie, the next night she came over. She looked interestedly down at him, faintly embarrassed, like a teacher pretending to be solicitous to a backward pupil.

'Keeps me going,' said Keith, leaning forward and turning up the television.

'I wanted to ask you about pointing brick,' she said, 'I want to make a dustbin shelter. I thought I might try to do it myself.'

He viewed her sceptically. 'There's not a lot to it. You mix up the mortar. Stack the bricks.'

'I want to do it properly. I want to find out all I can, I understand there's a knack to stacking bricks.'

He was filled with inexplicable rage but his face remained impassive. He got out a piece of paper and began to draw a diagram for her.

'It's a matter of checking the measurements and getting the levels right working from the foundations.'

Laurie blinked, nodded and took the piece of paper. 'Thanks, that's a great help,' she said.

'What am I?' he raged to Kay. 'They look at me. They don't see a person. No. All they see is a walking manual for all the donkey jobs no one in their right mind wants to do themselves.'

'Laurie respects you as a craftsman.' Kay banged down the plates on the dining bar. 'Why shouldn't she ask you?'

'Well, let her try it,' he muttered darkly. 'Let's see how quickly she develops the "knack".'

'I really don't see why you're so touchy about it . . .'

'I'm *touchy*,' he said, ' 'cos I make my living out of doing the donkey jobs for dumb middle-class women . . .' He slumped on the bar stool just as his beans on toast arrived.

'Well, if she can't do it, she'll pay you to do it,' said Kay. 'Anyway, there's plenty more brick walls in the world. One thing you can be sure of, there'll never be a shortage of brick walls, however many women build their own.'

This was of no consolation to Keith. They ate in silence. The truth of the matter was, he felt robbed of his dignity when his skills were adopted by a dilettante for a hobby. Dilettante – the word was his favourite for Laurie. It had bounced about the walls of the little council flat so frequently of late that Kay had been obliged to look it up.

As he ate Keith consoled himself with the thought of Laurie, owl-like, with her silver trowel smearing the mortar on like cake icing and all her bricks out of true.

Walking to work at six a.m. on Tuesday, humming to himself, admiring the apple blossom of Chesterton Road, he passed the run-down facade of Laurie's Victorian house. To the fore, conspicuously fresh, a newly cemented, perfectly square, red-brick dustbin shelter. He stopped and examined the workmanship. It couldn't be faulted. He felt like kicking it. He grunted and walked on, but he had stopped humming.

The next blow that fell was that Kay wanted to go to Munich for a week. Another of Laurie's bright-spark ideas.

'What is it? A holiday?' he asked.

'No,' she said, her brow furrowing, 'it's a sort of conference.'

He spent the next week trying to puzzle out what anyone could possibly want to confer with Kay about.

Keith understood on a rational level that it was only right Kay should be free to do other things outside of their life together. He expected to himself. And yet, every time it came to a note on the message pad or watching her cheerily waving goodbye in her oily dungarees, he felt a pang of betrayal. It was more than an ill-defined sense of resentment now. It was turning into something more general and more specific. The general was a feeling that his friends' wives did not feel the need to prove themselves by building cars. The specific focused on Laurie and Sally.

He resented the articulate middle-class women who greeted him politely as if he were some eccentric feature of Kay's life arrangements, some irrelevant appendage. They always seemed relieved when he left, anxious to get on with important business.

He viewed the piled back copies of *Spare Rib* with loathing. More than irritating him, the magazine actually filled him with an indefinable niggle of fear. Pages of strident, illegible text in dayglo red, sizzling against a black background, dancing in his head. At first he had concentrated his scorn on the layout of the rag, then he had turned his attention to the text. The new ones had a different layout and, being legible, were even more alarming. The same views or variations were laid out in sensible, even columns, as though this might make the content less outrageous. Lesbians declaiming their right to function sexually in the WRACs. That was one he cherished. He insisted on discussing these articles with Kay point to point. 'No, listen, look, we'll be serious then . . . so this woman achieves her lifelong ambition of becoming a Coldstream Guard,' and, 'So this woman wanted to be a barrister and she couldn't. *I* wanted to be a barrister and *I* couldn't.'

'You never wanted to be a barrister,' Kay objected mildly as she sat there, that evening, patching her trousers.

14

'No. And d'you know why?' He stabbed his finger in the air. She shook her head, mystified. 'Because I *couldn't* be a barrister, and it never crossed my mind to be because things aren't arranged that way, so I *knew* I couldn't.' He glared triumphantly at her. 'So am I discriminated against?'

Kay cocked her head on one side. 'Yes,' she said.

He nodded excitedly. 'Well, there you are. That's my point,' he said and sat down. But the victory was rather empty under the circumstances.

After a while, she spoke mildly in the voice she might use to ask for a cup of tea. 'Just because . . . some men . . . are discriminated against . . . you know through education or whatever, doesn't mean women should hold back fighting *their* battles, does it?' She went on stitching without looking up.

Something snapped in Keith. She had never spoken that way before. In fact, it wasn't Kay's voice. It was the voice of her friends. He stared at her with the horror of something unnatural as though a child had been possessed with the croaking voice of the devil. And in that split second a buzzing filled his ears and he saw everything they'd built up drifting away. The car was the beginning. A tangible symbol of escape. And just as surely the trip to Munich was the end. She was thirty-three and she was having no fun. He saw Benjamin dressed for the winter in little mittens, his face pinched blue. He saw him pushing the child on a swing in the park, dragging him round the Science Museum, then delivering him back to her in some basement flat somewhere. He watched her, swallowing a lump in his throat because the whole prospect was so frightening. He decided, at that moment, there was still time to stop it happening.

When Sally typed the last dot on the thesis, she went straight out to a print shop and got it photostatted. She wanted to give a copy to Laurie. She felt very good about it.

Sally tripped up the steps to Laurie's place, gay as a lark. The woman from downstairs let her in. The dank hall was stacked with drum cases and amplifiers and bicycles. Laurie's door was open and the flat looked like it had been burgled and ransacked, but this was nothing unusual. All of Laurie's energies were channelled elsewhere. The flat had never been a priority and she hadn't even put up a shelf. Shelving was such a simple, unexacting task that she couldn't be bothered to do it. Her paperbacks rested on planks supported by stacked bricks. Sally found Laurie in the kitchen, amongst the usual debris of unwashed plates, with mouldy teabags littering the draining board like bedraggled mice. She had her head in the bowl, washing her hair.

'Hi,' she said, and flipped her wet hair up into a towel.

'How's things?' asked Sally, noticing she had a Tubigrip on one arm.

'Great,' said Laurie with false brightness. 'I'm thinking of taking a photographic course. I think I've got a good visual sense, don't you?' She rattled on without waiting for an answer. 'I mean I can do the black-and-white printing. It's colour I need to have a go at. And I suppose you just have to put a lot of rolls through the camera before you can really tell if you're something special or not. I'd quite like to go to Eritrea or somewhere. Photo-reportage, that sort of thing . . .'

This seemed to Sally to be a wilder scheme than usual. She followed Laurie through to the front room.

'What happened to your arm?' she asked.

'Oh, just a strain,' said Laurie, 'I mean I'm talking about a long-term aim rather than something I could do right now. But at least it would have some significance . . . I mean, building the car, that was fine, but it's done now, and I think, well I just think I ought to be making more of a statement . . . with my life . . .'

Sally nodded gravely. They talked around it. What was significant, what wasn't. Laurie had phases of talking this way. Most usually when things were going badly in her everyday affairs.

Finally, Sally said, 'Was the driving test cancelled, or did something go wrong?' Laurie looked vague. She walked to the window and pretended to look out, pensively.

'Oh, that,' she said, dismissively. 'No, I didn't pass. But then, it hardly matters. It's no great sweat. I get round most places on the bicycle.' Sally stared at her back.

'Oh what a shame,' said Sally. It seemed inadequate. She knew how much it meant to Laurie. She hesitated. 'So, what happened?'

'Oh, nothing much,' said Laurie, 'I just made one or two errors but they were enough for her not to pass me.'

'What did you do wrong?'

Laurie's shoulders twitched in a shrug. 'The usual. I forgot to check the mirror and signal before I manoeuvred, or I got it in the wrong order or something. I didn't observe a traffic light and . . . well, anyway . . . I just didn't pass,' she said flatly.

Laurie continued to avoid the word that she was having trouble with – failed. Sally groped for the right thing to say.

'Well, you'll be better prepared next time . . .'

'No, I don't think I'll bother,' she said. 'Who needs to drive in London, anyway? It's just petrol and road tax and . . . wheel clamps, now.' Her face was still resolutely turned away but Sally had a strong idea she was struggling not to give way to tears.

'Look, come on, Laurie. It's only a driving test. It's not that important.'

'Yes,' said Laurie, her voice rather tremulous with emotion, 'it's silly really. It just seemed to mean so much, somehow. It seemed to have some . . . symbolic meaning . . . for me over and above what it should have had. Actually that was probably the trouble.' It ended on a sob. 'It was so mortifying!' Sally frowned, puzzled. Hundreds of people had failed their driving tests. It wasn't *that* mortifying, surely.

'I mean, I did forget to signal before the manoeuvre but . . .' Laurie turned and struggled to meet Sally's eye. 'But it was where I did it.'

Tugged by the tragic misery of Laurie's face, Sally went over and put her arms around her. Laurie was normally so brittle and strong that it would, in the usual run of things, be quite unthinkable. She began to sob out the awful story. Sally couldn't catch much but she thought she heard her say 'Shepherd's Bush roundabout' and then she distinctly heard her say 'Multi-car pileup'.

'How many cars?' asked Sally after a while, straining to believe that she'd heard aright, and yet wanting to make it sound natural and casual as though it happened on everyone's driving test. Laurie moved away, cross with herself for breaking down, searched for a tissue.

'Five,' she said, settling for a corner of the curtain. 'Six if you count the one that just had a bent wing.'

Sally stared at her, unable to think of the right diplomatic thing to say.

'Well, what did the test instructor say?'

'Oh, she was too busy attending to the casualty.'

'Was anyone badly hurt?' asked Sally, shocked.

'No. Just shock,' said Laurie, recovering herself now. 'Apparently there was a test case recently and the learner driver lost. I might be liable . . .'

Sally was stumped. She looked so perplexed that Laurie began to laugh.

'I mean, I didn't just fail,' she said, tears gumming up her eyelashes, 'I failed in the most spectacular way possible.' She paced the room. 'Anyway, I think Munich's off for me, whatever.'

'Yes,' said Sally, slowly. 'But don't you think a rest – getting away – might do you good?' It wasn't self-interest so much as the fact that Laurie seemed so shaken and off-balance, so unlike her normal self.

'It's not that,' said Laurie, 'I suppose it's just . . . well this has kind of knocked my self-esteem. I think I ought to do something very positive. Being driven around, half asleep, feeling like a parcel, it's not going to do a lot for me, frankly, is it?'

'No,' said Sally, 'I suppose not.'

And a little later, Sally picked up her thesis, lying unnoticed on the chair, and it suddenly looked very un-significant to her and she wondered why she had felt so excited only a few hours before.

Sally passed by the travel agents on the way to Kilburn High Road. She collected as many brochures as she could find for the Rhine route to Munich. She wanted to give Kay an idea of the possible stops along the way. She called in at the mini-cab office where Kay worked afternoons. It was a tiny, sordid tip. The walls had the impermanency of an unfinished set and were papered with peeling vinyl that bore unpleasant green flowers as big as cartwheels. It stank of stale cigars, melting plastic and dog's breath. Whether the melting plastic smell came from the tired fifties bar stools, the Second World War aircraft seats or the overheating TV that bellowed out from daybreak to the end of broadcasting, nobody knew. As for the other, the dog had long died but its secretions haunted the stuffing of its favourite spots. Kay wished the parrot would die too. Today, the air hummed with a special piquancy because it was seventy-five in the street and ninety inside. The fan puffed ineffectually, swivelling as fast as it could on its thin stalk, with no chance to keep up and no chance at all of winning. Kay sat wedged in her usual position between the four middle-aged men who were her colleagues. As usual, Sally felt disorientated as she walked in. It was the noise converging from all directions. The radio receivers, the cartoon on the box, phones ringing, the kettle whistling on the gas stove and the old photostat machine wheezing as it gathered strength to memorise the copy and spit out the duplicate. A wizened woman, who never spoke, operated the devious monster. It gave off a green light that Kay swore was phosphorous.

'Hi,' said Sally, 'I got the brochures.' She dumped them beside the tin lid ashtray with its usual complement of chewing gum and teabags. 'I think the alpine route sounds a great idea and it won't take that much longer . . .'

Kay had a dull lethargy about her. Her expression hardly changed. Sally knew something was up.

'Gamma five. I got an airport run fourteen-thirty. D'you want it?' She flicked down the switch, looked up wearily, dropped her voice. 'Can't come, can I?'

Sally stared at her.

'He says he'll have the locks changed if I go.'

'But . . .' Sally could hardly credit it. He seemed such a decent, reasonable person. 'He's known for *weeks* . . .'

Kay grimaced. Sally pressed on. 'But I thought he was okay about it . . .'

'Well, he was. *Then*.'

A muffled voice came over the intercom. She put her mouth to the microphone.

'Well, d'you think you'd like to come back to base at some point, if it's not inconvenient?'

Sally watched her unhappily. Kay had been so looking forward to it. It was a real blow.

A low fruity voice came back over the radio: 'Depends what you're offering, darling.'

Kay scowled as he cut out. 'Nope,' she said finally, looking up at Sally, 'I think we can definitely say he's not okay about it.'

Sally hesitated, concerned, wanting to ask more, but it was understood with them that they never spoke about Kay's marriage apart from pleasantries. 'Is everything all right?' she asked, which was as far as she could go.

'Yes,' said Kay, bristling slightly, aware that Sally was looking too closely. She busied herself with a notepad. 'You can take Laurie, anyway. It's no big deal,' she said, choosing to misinterpret the concern. 'She'll pass her test. She's bound to. It'll all work out.'

'That's not the point,' said Sally, quietly. She thought now was hardly the time to break the other bombshell.

'I can't afford to see the bloody point, can I?' said Kay unhappily.

Chapter 2

They had the week to think about things, and, after a series of phone calls and much intense discussion, they agreed to meet at Kay's on Monday evening, since she was not allowed out. Sally came out of the grim aerosolled lift and walked along the anonymous corridor on the fourteenth floor. It wasn't much of a life for Kay, she brooded, the three of them jammed in a concrete box. The panorama from the window was breathtaking, fairy lights pinpointing in the black, but it was also disconcerting. It was a long way for a packet of sugar. She wondered how many people had taken the direct route down.

Her own flat was on the first floor of a three-storey house, and the Victorians had known the sensible limit for housing creatures who couldn't fly.

Keith was surly and shamefaced. 'They're in there,' he said, tipping his head contemptuously at the small front room. He went off purposefully to the kitchen where he was making kitchen cupboards in preparation for the new Wonder cooker he'd just ordered. This was part of The Plan. He was throwing himself into his self-appointed tasks with manic single-mindedness. The plan was to improve the Nest. He was fitting new brass curtain rails, fitting Regency doorknobs, doggedly designing a new boudoir for marital intimacy that had just stopped taking place. But he had a sense it wasn't working. Instead of getting on with the F-Plan Diet book he had bought her, she was often, lately, caught out stuffing doughnuts, sugar dusted round her mouth, cream oozing out in voluptuous wiggles. She seemed to have given up on her appearance and the carrot rinse was fading from her once geometric layers. The more feverish his woodwork, the more dull-eyed and defeated she became. He took up his saw and tape measure with determination and tried to put the problem from his mind. He felt a fierce dart of joy that Laurie had failed her driving test.

'Is he all right?' asked Sally, as she settled in the room.

'Yes,' said Kay. 'He's just feeling defensive, that's all. You've gotta make allowances.'

Laurie avoided Sally's eye.

'How far have you got?' she asked, plonking herself down in a chair and nearly impaling her leg on the Kiddi-Car.

'Well, it's up to five pounds already,' Kay warned.

'Read it out,' she begged.

'Trip to Munich. Then the dates,' Kay read. 'German-speaking woman. Must be mechanically-minded driver. Preferably vegetarian. Non-smoker.' She looked up. 'How's that?' Personally, she thought it was a slightly tall order.

Sally had listened intently, rather glazed. She was so set on going now that she considered striking out non-smoker, but then, she reconsidered, she didn't want to sit in a moving ashtray.

'Yuh,' she said, decidedly. 'Sounds pretty watertight.' And then as an afterthought, 'I will *get* someone all right?'

Laurie took it from Kay and folded it up. 'Honestly, Sally, everyone I know who's put in an ad got at *least* thirty replies. You're more likely to be overwhelmed.' True, that was the Lonely Hearts, but even so . . .

She got the listings magazine on Thursday and, sure enough, there was the advert. It pleased her to see it in type. It looked so official, as though setting it down in black and white guaranteed that the trip would go ahead. She began to wait for the post with mounting anticipation, and by the time the week was up, she was conditioned to stir herself even at the sound of a soap-powder coupon dropping on the mat.

When it arrived, she was fingers and thumbs opening it. A small azure envelope plopped out first. She tipped the brown one up, but no others followed. Disappointed, she poked about inside, as though a plain manila envelope could have a secret compartment. She sat down at the kitchen table and read the letter slowly over

22

her muesli. It was distinctly odd. For one thing, the woman's hand was disappointingly unformed, and, for another, the stress on her gayness was slightly alarming. It wasn't until she reached the spidery scrawl of the signature that the reason for this became clear to her. It was signed Harry Hammell. Otherwise, he was admirably qualified. He just wasn't a woman.

She rang Laurie at the metal workshop.

'I'd say the world was full of mechanically-minded women who *don't* want to go to Germany next week.'

'Really?' Laurie shouted against the deafening din of the arc-welding equipment. 'Well, how many are there?'

'There's only one,' she said, staring at the thin blue sheet. 'And it's signed Harry.'

'Ah,' said Laurie. There was a moment's decent silence. 'Now that *is* a snag.'

'He's gay,' said Sally. 'I don't suppose there's any conceivable possibility . . .' She tailed off. An unknown man alone in a car for extended periods of time on lonely stretches of roads. 'No,' they both said together.

'We'll have to think of something,' said Laurie decisively. Sally thought the 'we' was very comforting but it probably didn't mean a lot. They met at lunchtime and wandered down Portobello market. Laurie said she'd ring around some people but London emptied at this time of year, and anyway Sally had to leave on Thursday week.

They bumped into Kay by accident. She was doing her shopping and didn't seem very pleased to see them. She had had an irritating day, and she was beginning, in some dim reach of her brain, to see things as Keith constantly presented them to her. Maybe her troubles *did* stem from Sally and Laurie. Certainly she had been happy enough before that fateful evening class.

The cake-icing class had been over-subscribed and she had been siphoned into the silkscreen group. She had been perfectly content squeegeeing ill-formed Snoopies on to a cot cover until the fateful night when Laurie hovered at her elbow and offered to hose down her screen. It was only after that that she had begun to

23

feel discontented. And what with the self-defence classes and then the jeep, maybe she *had* been neglecting Keith. It was as though new ideas had pressed in and awakened some old spark, but that spark was not really appropriate for someone with responsibilities. Now she tried to throw herself into Sally's problem, while still keeping an eye out for bargains in the vegetable line.

'I can go on my own,' Sally was insisting.

'It's much too far,' said Laurie.

'Look, why don't you see this bloke,' said Kay. 'He might be all right. He doesn't sound too bad.' She felt responsible for Sally's predicament. 'I can't see it makes *that* much difference.'

Laurie gave Sally one of her knowing looks. Kay intercepted it and turned on her sharply. 'It's no good the pair of you looking at me like I'm a . . . collaborator in the French resistance or something. I can't see 'em all as the enemy 'cos I happen to be married to one of 'em.'

Sally spoke slowly, not wanting to offend her, but needing to explain. 'I don't know,' she said. 'Going to a women's thing. It doesn't feel right.' She was almost apologetic. 'I can't see how you can think one thing and do something else, really . . .'

'Apart from the fact he can't quite manage joined-up writing,' said Laurie flippantly. Sally winced.

'I thought you wanted a driver, not a literary genius,' said Kay. 'I just think if it's a choice of going or not going, you could give him a chance and *pretend* you've got an open mind.'

They walked along in silence for a moment.

Then Laurie said, 'But she hasn't.'

For a moment Sally felt much more in sympathy with poor beleaguered Kay and Keith than Laurie. She stared into some middle distance. Had she or hadn't she, she wondered as she mooched back to her flat. And under these circumstances was an open mind a good thing or a bad thing?

Harry was twenty minutes early. He located the ICA in an unlikely spot amongst some blind government buildings in the

Mall. It was a white, low-lying block, like a slab of impenetrable wedding cake. He walked up and down in front of it a few times, uneasy and uncomfortable in the borrowed suit. The shadows were black and geometric in the overhead sun. He fancied the building had an Egyptian flavour to it. A parched palm tree would have looked at home.

His spirits soared momentarily. Perhaps next week he'd be in a foreign country under a foreign sun. The suit was lightweight seersucker, white with blue stripes. This morning it had seemed just the thing – rather casual and devil-may-care, a suit for someone used to travelling, crisp and cool and effortlessly elegant. Now he was not so sure. The sweat was trickling down his back and running a stream into the bunched fabric of the outsize waistband and he was increasingly aware of the way the trousers ballooned out at the knees and ended up lapping unwanted over his glistening brogues. An image of Andy Pandy in a white and blue one-piece kept humping into his mind unasked and he scowled as he felt his confidence ebbing. He swerved into the doorway before he could think better of it and lurched into the bookshop with a purposeful air. The assistants had the air of people who'd agreed to lower themselves to the task as a short-term favour and who found each contact with a customer unspeakably droll. They sparred roguishly with one another, letting out occasional hoots whilst keeping a weather eye on Harry's spade fingers as he leafed through creamy pages of text looking for pictures. Harry turned on his heels and made for the gents, his confidence ebbing to rock bottom.

George Orwell was right, he told himself bitterly as he quarrelled with the towel roller, it's something you give off in your pores and people have an infallible nose for it. He jutted his jaw at himself in the mirror. I may not have *class*, he told himself defiantly, but what I *do* have is boyish charm. At thirty-three this was a rare and useful tool to have in the kit. It had always served him well before and in *this* instance it was his only card. He had never been so determined about anything. He was *going* to Munich.

He strolled down the corridor. A long paper scroll was stretched along one wall, dotted all over with multi-coloured palm prints. The motto screamed GIVE A HAND TO POLAND. Someone thrust a choice of paint pots at him. He felt he *ought* to give a hand, but he couldn't see how it would actually *help*, whereas a navy-blue palm-print might actively hinder his own negotiations. He passed on. There was only one small misgiving. He had never tried the charm out on a feminist. In fact, he couldn't remember ever having met one before.

Sally was seated in an alcove, idly swabbing ketchup from the table with a serviette. She looked around her at the businessmen settled with newspapers and croissants. There was a table full of paint-splattered stagehands or artists, no doubt discussing burning matters of creativity. She toyed with her brown rice cake. There was no one who looked remotely as if he might have penned the rather quaint paragraphs in front of her on the ruled sheet of Basildon Bond.

The walls were hung with a travelling exhibition. She became aware that she was sitting under a lurid parody of a centrefold girl overprinted with the bold message:

> *Some Men Think Women*
> *Are Their Toys*
> *To Be Used, Played With*
> *Murdered And Thrown Away*
> *Like Candy Wrappers.*

Perhaps not the most auspicious greeting, she thought, considering a mental image of herself sitting under it looking completely humourless and fierce. She began to put her little Chinese ricepot back on the tray with the polythene cup of juice. Then she thought better of moving. It might be a bit strident but it was certainly true. She settled an even fiercer look on her face. Perhaps she could scare him off quickly. He would probably be a computer operator. She could hear herself already: 'Oh, that must be terribly interesting.'

'Yes, well, it's fascinating to those of us in the know.' She gave him a sort of nasal twang as he shifted forward in his tube-like blue serge suit. 'I don't know how much you know about systems analysis but are you familiar with the sort of advances that are going on now in microtechnology?' and she would smile encouragingly as he got himself into his stride. What was she doing seeing him at all? The whole thing was a polite charade, a waste of time brought about because of her own lack of firmness and this man's impertinent insistence. She settled on a look of uncompromising disdain. It was as she sneered myopically into the middle distance that Harry plucked up courage to sidle into the food bar and assess the situation. He approached her as though she were a rare butterfly, his scrolled copy of the *Guardian* held up like a challenge.

'Sally?'

She tapped her own *Guardian* and smiled reluctantly.

'Harry.'

They shook hands.

'Sorry about the red paint,' she said, 'I just couldn't get it all off.' She heartily wished she hadn't stuck it in the pot.

Harry sat down relieved. At least the hair wasn't cropped and she'd left off the dungarees. She had a rather grim expression, but he put this down to shyness. After all, it was an artificial situation.

'Well, where shall I start?' he asked with a diffident smile.

She was rather golden, now he looked at her. She had the creamy skin, the even features of the upper-middle classes and the stillness of someone who'd been brought up in a house with a bit of space.

'Mm. Well, anywhere really,' she said. 'Er . . . I mean I think I ought to just say it's still all very much in the air . . .'

He nodded sagely. 'Yes, of course. I mean you don't want to get stuck with someone you can't get on with. Well, that's why I'm here, isn't it? We've just gotta talk round one another a bit.'

He looked at her for approval, took the slightly dazed look for just that and proceeded to get his facts in order and lay the picture out.

'Well, the thing is, I'm doing this Open University course in my spare time and, like, well it's mostly weekends and evenings, you know, because I don't get a lot of time – of course there are summer seminars you can go to but I haven't seemed to be able to fit those into the schedule so far . . .'

She had no idea where this was leading but it gave her a chance to examine his face as he struggled on with the painstaking detail. He had a large, honest, open face; very mobile features. His nose had a slightly comic tilt and the eyes were big, brown and spaniel-like. She supposed he was in his early thirties. The suit was something of a puzzle. It suggested a down-at-heel art-school lecturer or a journalist whereas the person in it looked more like a lorry driver.

'And of course, then I've been doing this office job for the last couple of months and you don't get much chance to keep up on the homework . . .'

'What are you studying?'

'History of Architecture at the moment. And, you know, like you get course credits if you visit the place like, in this case Germany you see. Er, and I chose to do Ludwig's Schlosses . . .'

'What made you pick that?' she asked suddenly.

He sat back in his chair, beginning to relax. 'Oh, I don't know, I suppose if I think back I read a bit on the back of a cornflake packet or something when I was a kid and it just sort of stuck in me mind. There's something about Ludwig that just fired my imagination.'

He saw she was drinking it in and ventured to give a little poetry: 'You know, that megalomania, that vision . . . and the palaces . . . monuments to this monumental ego . . .

'I mean it may seem late in life,' he went on, 'but there again my education was a bit truncated. I used to read a lot but there's only so much you can get from books. I used to get in off night shift and just fall asleep. Then just recently I thought the old brain needs a kick start now and then. D'you know what I mean?'

'I do,' she said.

'What worries me now,' he said, looking pensively across the room, 'is the fact that I've fallen behind on a couple of assignments. Well, I can maybe catch those up . . .' He shrugged as though he were really talking to himself. 'But the clincher is the thesis really. If I can really turn out a good one . . . I mean I don't wanna just pass, that's the trouble. A thing's not worth doing unless you excel, you know what I mean?'

Sally was nodding, taken up for a moment with his inner struggles. Against her better judgment she was beginning to feel a flicker of interest in him. She admired people who struggled to get themselves an education when all the odds were against them. And the more she looked at Harry's rather soulful face, the more plain it was to her that the odds had always been against him. It was just something he radiated. It *did* seem a rather obscure subject for a thesis.

'And of course for that I really need to make the trip. See the palaces. Drink in the atmosphere. Take some snaps.' He gave a self-deprecating smile, and took a breath as though what he was about to say was an effort: 'It really is very important to me.'

Sally opened her mouth to speak, recalling that she was about to fail him dismally.

He sensed as much and anticipated; 'So that's why, when I saw the ad . . .' He was fumbling in his pocket now, drew out a dog-eared clipping. 'It just seemed like a godsend. And when I saw the dates coincided with me holiday period it just seemed too good to be true.'

'The only thing,' she started.

'German-speaking.' He stabbed the advert. 'Well I've been learning it for ages. Mechanically-minded. Five years Ford trim shop speaks for itself. That was two years on the Cortina and three on the Estate,' he added confidentially for her information. 'Vegetarian.' He began to check them off in a more cursory way as though running through a shopping list. 'Given up the fags . . .'

Sally came to her senses and moved restlessly in her seat. It was painful to watch him when she knew categorically he wasn't going anywhere.

'And then it hit me. The stumbling block. Woman. But I thought – give it a go like, it might be negotiable, and then . . .' He tapped his badge significantly. She peered at it. It said 'Glad to be

29

gay'. 'It's not as though I'd be any trouble that way. I couldn't care if you were an Antarctic seal . . . except it might get in the way of the driving.'

'Look . . . but that's the thing,' she said, butting in with difficulty, 'I'm not sure that it really *is* negotiable.'

He stopped in his tracks. 'Oh, I see,' he said flatly, 'I thought because we met, like . . . I stood a bit of a chance . . .' Then, as an afterthought, rather accusingly, 'That's why I put me suit on.' He looked so crestfallen it might have been comic in other circumstances.

'Well, it's only that you were so insistent on the phone,' she said rather desperately. 'I mean I suppose it's my fault. I should have made it clearer.' No, that wasn't right. She *had* made it clear. 'I mean I said no on the phone and you just somehow got it twisted round and then I felt obliged . . .' She trailed off lamely at sight of his expression. 'I really did want a woman.'

He shifted restlessly in his seat. 'Look, I don't want to force myself on anyone. I can see you're on the spot. You don't want to buy a pig in a poke.'

Sally protested, horribly embarrassed, 'No, that's not it at all.'

Harry stood up suddenly with immense dignity. 'It's fine,' he said, waving it away with his hand. 'I can see I'm not your sort. It was good of you to take the time to have a look at me.' He tried a brave smile. 'I ought to be off. I'm sure you've got a lot more to see.'

She stared miserably at the highly polished table-top. He put his hand out to show no hard feelings, smiled warmly as if he understood.

'Look, I'll give you a ring,' she said, trying to master the situation. 'And let you know when I've . . .'

'Seen the others, yes.' He finished off the polite fiction. 'Well, nice to meet you anyway. Hope you enjoy the trip.' And he was gone.

She sat there for a little while feeling rather wrung out. Real feminists could handle these situations. Real feminists were clear and assertive. They saw manipulative manoeuvres, identified them for what they were and dealt with them in a direct, straightforward way, clearly stating their own needs. It came back to the argument with Kay. What right had she to call herself a feminist when she constantly thought one way and acted in another?

She walked to Charing Cross Road and browsed in Collett's. She bought a couple more books on assertion therapy. Even as she leafed through them, she found herself thinking that her own five years of further education had been acquired with no effort at all; she had just accepted them as her due.

She trudged slowly up Ladbroke Grove towards her flat, her spirits at a very low ebb. So that was it. There would be no trip. It was too long a journey to do alone and besides it would be no pleasure. She supposed she could fly, but that defeated the whole object. The smell of soup was blowing from the social services and a man was standing under the struts of the bridge shouting at the sky, his voice filling the late afternoon streets with a curious naked hollowness. By the church, someone shuffled towards her, muttering under his breath, pyjamas underneath his clothes. He wore two mismatching oven gloves and carried laundry bags. She realised that her problem really was very insignificant, her thwarted plans very trivial. She resolved to let the thing go gracefully.

She settled into her flat and drooped. Since she was going nowhere, she made up her mind to clean the flat. She vacuumed throughout, scrubbed the bathroom and attended to the plants. That done, she sat down in the spotless space and tapped her fingers. It was a warm evening, and she was filled with a deep nostalgic longing for something, she didn't know what. The whole summer stretched before her like an extremely boring book that she'd read before. This was how she would spend it, flitting from the front room to the back room, in and out of the bedroom, throwing up the windows and letting someone else's curry drift in on the breeze.

And, against her better judgment, she found herself thinking about the man she'd met in the café, who was trying to better himself. The letter lay discarded on the table. His writing was like half-joined-up spiders and she found it rather touching.

Before she could think better of it, she picked up the receiver and began to dial the number scrawled at the top of the crumpled sheet. Someone answered. It sounded, as before, like a coinbox in an uncarpeted hall. The message taker was a slavic person with no second language and only the two words, 'Oo's there?' which he repeated several times in answer to her name. She had an uncomfortable feeling this might be a psychiatric hospital. She said Harry's name emphatically a few times, and when the ghostly parrot-like repetition turned round to 'Ammell oo?' she had a sure feeling that this was Not Meant To Be. She was just about to replace the receiver when she heard footsteps racing towards the phone, and then Harry's voice panting at the other end. 'Yes?' he gasped.

'It's Sally Francis,' she said.

'You're going to take me?' His voice was alive with delighted surprise.

She gave him the details in a businesslike way. He gave her an address.

'You won't regret it, Sally,' he assured her earnestly, and was still assuring her after she'd signed off and was replacing the phone.

Well, that was that. She sat back and stared at her pale reflection in the mirror and wondered what on earth she'd done.

Chapter 3

The day dawned, crisp and clear. She drove up and down the back streets of Paddington in the early morning light, looking for the address. She had found the number all right but in a terrace of extremely unsavoury-looking bed-and-breakfast hotels. Sixty-four bore a flickering perspex sign hanging lopsided from its rusty chain. The Eros Hotel. There were two inmates seated on the steps. The more grizzled of the two had pyjamas on under his clothes and was muttering to himself. This *can't* be it, she thought. He had made no mention of a hotel. She was about to get back in the jeep and drive around some more when the swing doors exploded open. And there was Harry, smiling like a cheshire cat, laden down with luggage like a pack donkey.

'Sally!' he shouted and bounded down the steps towards her with undisguised excitement. He was hauling a battered haversack and sleeping bag and was hung about with a motley collection of bulging grips and naval kitbags. Did the nylon sack hold a tent?

He stopped, taken aback at the sight of the jeep. He stood and appraised it. He had imagined they were going in a normal car. He became aware that she was awaiting some reaction.

'It's a great colour,' he said.

She smiled happily. It *was* a great colour. Like a boiled sweet. She threw up the flap at the back and began to stack his ill-assorted luggage beside her two prim cases.

'We built it,' she said. 'It's mostly Ford Escort parts.' She was bent double trying to pack it neatly without blocking the back window. She didn't see his change of expression.

'You built it?'

There seemed to be such a lot of luggage. There was also a primus, assorted cutlery and a small tin kettle in a catfood box.

33

'It took about three weeks.'

Harry nodded thoughtfully, eyeing the car afresh. He framed his next question with tact.

'I see. Have you er . . . built any cars before?'

She looked up, surprised. There was a hint of asperity in her voice: 'No, this was our first.'

He began to look at it more carefully, running his hand along the sill as he scrutinised the bodywork. Peering in the window.

'Well, it's good for a first effort,' he said cautiously.

Sally turned round to give a sharp reply and found herself flanked by a large, fat man who had shambled down the steps unremarked. He transfixed her with a lascivious china-blue eye, swaying backwards slightly to keep her in focus. He addressed himself across her head to Harry:

'Ah, you always fall on your feet, you lucky dog. I wish I was going with you.'

Harry groaned inwardly. Just the sort of image he didn't want to present.

Sally watched with a strained smile as Harry allowed himself to be pressed warmly into the ample flesh of the big man's stained shirtfront.

'See you, mate,' said Harry, extricating himself at the earliest opportunity from the blast of rank whisky fumes.

'I think we should go,' said Sally in a clipped voice and she got into the jeep. Her brain was racing. It was a mistake. It was a terrible mistake. Laurie was absolutely right. There were any number of well-tried reasons why she should not be in a car alone with a man whom she knew nothing about, and they were all flooding at her now in lurid headlines. Harry piled in beside her and she started the engine. The motley group of individuals now gathered on the steps waved as the car pulled out.

There was little traffic at that time of the morning. It wasn't until they were spinning along a deserted Park Lane that Sally unpursed her lips.

'Was that your boyfriend?' she ventured in a non-committal tone.

34

Harry looked up from his private thoughts, shocked.

'Of course not,' he said. 'That was the doorman.'

He was sitting hunched and tense, taking in the dials in front of him, watching the fuel gauge nervously, looking around surreptitiously at what appeared to be pop-rivets in the chassis, assessing its roadworthiness. It felt ominously flimsy in top gear. He wondered if that was right. Shouldn't a jeep feel more solid? Had it all been tested properly? Sally looked quite a fragile woman. In fact she looked like bone china. Had they tightened all the bolts? He wondered if there was a tactful way to ask about the M.O.T.

'So what made you decide on a car then?' he asked lightly.

Sally stared grimly ahead. 'We were going to build a sewing machine but they're not very good on corners,' she said.

'Still, I don't suppose this is very good at running up curtains.' He looked at her for a reaction but she didn't smile. 'You built the engine and all that?'

She nodded tersely.

'Well, that's very impressive.' He wished he'd had a better chance to look at the thing.

'Is it, why?' she asked coldly.

He could sense the warning tone. 'No reason. I'm just saying I'm impressed, that's all.' He tapped his fingers on his teeth. 'Got a fire extinguisher?'

'Yes, there's a first-aid kit in the back as well. Carry on the way you are and you might be wise to keep it handy.' She spoke in a low undertone and he wondered if he'd heard her right. Her eyes were firmly fixed on the road and her jaw was clamped. It was his first intimation that things might be tricky.

'Okay. There's no need to get touchy. We don't want to get touchy with one another if we want to be mates.'

Sally didn't want to be his mate. She was already wondering if it would be too pointed to clamp her Sony Walkman on, and they were only at the Elephant and Castle.

But, once clear of the gloomy decay of Deptford, and through some of the smugger towns of Kent, the mood lightened. It was motorway from now on and open countryside and sky. It was

35

impossible not to feel some of the old childhood excitement at going on a trip.

They stopped in a layby and rolled the top back. The sun was beating down and the air was fragrant with pollen. At the garage, he paid for the petrol with a fistful of notes and came back with a box of supplies – sweets and juice and some cans of beer. He offered to take over the driving. She said she'd rather do one long stint.

'I like this little jeep,' he said, after a while. The wind was cool and refreshing. They were doing eighty in top. Now that he was getting used to the thing, it didn't feel so unstable. 'I feel like I'm in an American road-movie. Driving fast in an open-top car. Can of beer in my hand and a –' He was about to say a beautiful girl beside me, but he stopped himself. She might think he meant her, whereas it was just an abstract. She wasn't exactly beautiful. She was rather a cold fish and reminded him of a schoolteacher.

He picked up the guidebook and began to browse idly through it, snuffling occasionally. It had been translated from the German and some of the sentence constructions were stiff and ungainly. He read one out loud in a mock German accent:

'The Chermans are great lovers of nature. It is a deepseated national characteristic. The sight of land laid waste or forest despoiled shocks them profoundly.' He looked up. 'Oh yeah? Didn't worry too much about Coventry, did they?'

'We didn't worry too much about Dresden,' she answered mechanically.

Unabashed, he persisted with his grating impression of an SS officer:

'Olympic stadium of ingenious construction, involving one hundred and ten miles of steel wire . . . Well,' he broke off, 'well, they've had a bit of practice with high perimeter fencing . . .'

Sally gave a tight-lipped smile. She had overlooked the possibility that she might be treated to xenophobic jokes the whole way across Germany.

Harry carried on reading, rather bored now, just picking out items to fill the air:

'Neuschwanstein Castle. Built by Ludwig the Second . . .' He pulled himself up short, suddenly aware that here was his specialist subject and he was required to comment. 'Oh, that's interesting. I think you'll find that's the one where he hung himself.'

Sally's brow furrowed. Her concentration faltered and then broke. She turned round to him, utterly disconcerted. 'He *drowned*.'

Harry felt a light sweat break out on his upper lip; a prickling sensation moved up the back of his neck.

'Er, yes.' He avoided her eye. 'But he tried to hang himself first, I think you'll find . . .'

At that moment, if all the electrical impulses of their combined brain activity could have been harnessed they might have powered a small sawmill.

She made a decision and turned sharply off the motorway into the slip road towards the cafeteria. He watched her with foreboding as she got out and strode towards the phone box. He let himself out at a more leisurely pace and ambled round to the back of the car. He surveyed his wealth of ill-assorted baggage.

'Kay, it's Sally,' she breathed anxiously down the receiver. 'I'm not at all sure about all this.'

Kay had to shout above the manic chaos of the minicab office. 'Where are you?'

'A little way from Dover.'

'What's wrong?'

'Well, it's hard to say exactly but he lives in a really seedy doss-house and, well, this may seem a funny question but, did Ludwig the Second try to hang himself?'

Kay was slightly nonplussed.

'Is it important?'

'Yes,' said Sally impatiently.

'Well, let me see,' said Kay. 'Who would know?' She surveyed the lumpen goons she worked with. Bill, with his big bottom spreading over his undersized stool. The pips went and Sally pressed in more coins urgently. Then Kay remembered.

'Well, wouldn't *he* know? I thought he was studying it. Ask him.'

37

'You'd think he'd know, wouldn't you?' said Sally triumphantly.

But then a little seed of doubt sprung up in her mind. Perhaps he *had* tried to hang himself. Perhaps this was the sort of abstruse and useless knowledge that one learned from a course of the History of Architecture.

Kay couldn't understand the problem but she understood the tone of panic in Sally's voice. 'Look,' she said sensibly in the voice of her mother, 'if you've got any doubts whatsoever cut your losses. It's too risky.'

'That's what I was thinking,' said Sally cautiously. She watched him out of the corner of her eye. He seemed to have all his luggage out on the tarmac. She wondered what he was up to.

'Is he paying his way all right?'

'Yes,' said Sally, 'that's what makes it difficult.' The box of supplies was sitting on the front seat like an accusation.

'Well, don't worry about that. You'll pay him back his petrol money but best sort things out here and now. Don't take any chances.'

Sally stood in the kiosk for a long moment after she'd put down the phone. She was trying to gather up her resolve. Then she swung firmly out.

He didn't appear to be repacking the mountain of baggage in a more rational way, as she'd assumed. He just stood looking at it as though it was an insoluble puzzle.

'Harry,' she said evenly.

He looked up vaguely but avoided her eye.

'It's not working out, is it?' He picked up the haversack and levered his arms into the straps. 'You don't have to say anything. I can tell.' He picked up two more bags and slung them from the crook of his elbow. 'I can hitch back. It's no problem.' He could manage the naval kitbag and the duffel bag but there was still a box, another grip and a sleeping bag. Sally eyed him uneasily as he tried to manoeuvre them all. He took in her strained expression. 'Look, we're strangers. You don't owe me anything.' He said it in a kindly, off-hand way to let her off the hook.

'It's only a matter of stacking the gear right.' He turned round heavily with all his encumbrances and stooped forward so that she confronted his backpack. 'Could you just load the lilo on the top and maybe stuff the primus down the pocket?'

She picked up the lilo. Stood there impotently holding it, staring miserably at his proffered back as he waited patiently like some old docile donkey. She let the lilo drop. Picked up the primus wearily and lobbed it in the back of the car.

'Oh, let's just get there, shall we?' She turned on her heel and slammed into the driving seat.

'Are you sure?' he asked hopefully.

She started the engine. 'I'm sure,' she said through clenched teeth.

He began hurriedly stuffing his luggage into the back of the jeep. He managed to clamber into his seat just as she was accelerating off. He smiled trustingly at her but she kept her eyes mulishly ahead. She screeched out of the services and back on to the motorway that led off the map.

I'll take him, she thought, but I'm damned if I have to talk to him. So they sat in silence as the fields sped by in bright washes of broad colour.

Harry kept fidgeting. What was golden to the next man was cruel and unusual punishment with Harry. He liked conversation and he had a feeling it was going to be withheld the whole way to Munich. After an intolerable, yawning half-hour of it, he ventured a pleasantry.

'Nice seeing a bit of countryside after London, like, isn't it?'

She nodded dourly.

'Do you like country?' he enquired, as though the two thoughts were connected, which they weren't.

'Mmm,' she answered vaguely, lost in the mesmerised state brought on by staring at a whizzing white line. He leaned forward enthusiastically.

'Great. I can see we're going to get on. I've got quite a collection.' And he slotted in a cassette.

The repetitive twanging wail of Kenny Rogers began its pre-dictable trajectory across the heartstrings. Sally's eyes faltered from the wheel to Harry's hand slapping his thigh, to his knee moving up and down.

> That's why I asked her
> My place or your place,
> I hope I'm not outa line.
> I asked the wrong thing
> to just the right woman this time.
> She knew a hotel
> She even knew a name we could sign.
> Yeah, the cheaper the grapes are
> the sweeter the taste of the wine.

Sally closed her eyes and gave a deep and heartfelt mental groan.

Chapter 4

They found themselves in the ferry queue at Dover at about midday. Sally was fidgety and kept looking at her watch. They had no conversation because Harry seemed lost in some private reverie. He got out of the car and stared up at the cliffs. He tried to take a photograph of a seagull. He said it was the biggest seagull he had ever seen. She said they were all that big but one didn't often see them standing up that close. He smothered himself in suntan lotion and leant back against the car. It seemed an eternity before they were finally summoned to roll on.

Harry stood on the deck amongst the holidaymakers watching the white cliffs pull away. The wash from the ship created a vast foam V that linked them still to the white walls of chalk. The seagulls swooped and scavenged. They made a mournful noise.

It was quite choppy and the juddering sent waves of nausea through her body. Her limbs felt curiously heavy and her head felt light. She wasn't good on boats and she wanted to go in. Harry stood, still deep in thought, leaning on the rail, impressing the majestic image on his retina.

She said rather impatiently, 'Do you want to take a photo?'

'There's some things you can't photograph,' he said broodily.

She looked curiously at his head and wondered what was going on in it. He was humming quietly to himself. It sounded like 'There'll be bluebirds over . . .'

He was thinking about the fragmented picture of Dunkirk that his father had passed on to him. He was seeing the little boats.

A crowd of German children were jostling against her and someone had a telephoto lens pressed into her hip like a gun. She turned: 'When you've had your fill of the exotic ambience you'll find me in the drinks deck in the warm.'

A flicker of irritation crossed his face. 'Okay. It's all right for you. You've been.'

'Been where?'

'Abroad.'

'Well, haven't you?'

'No.'

There was a curious, brittle vulnerability about him as he spoke that warned her to press it no further. But it was inconceivable to Sally that anyone of his age could not have left the country of his birth even once.

'How old are you?'

'Thirty-three.'

'Weren't there any school trips?' As she said it, she despised herself for asking. Of course there hadn't been any school trips.

He didn't bother to answer but turned his face back to the shore.

'They've seen a lot of history, those cliffs,' he said finally.

'If I stand here much longer, they'll see me throwing up.'

He turned to her, immediately solicitous. 'Do you really feel sick? Are you okay?' He put his arm on her elbow and she felt the pressure of real concern.

'Yeah, I'm okay but I think I'll go down.'

She turned and walked away, disconcerted by the blast of unexpected warmth. It was akin to something she had felt before and forgotten about. She dismissed the thought almost instantly. If anything it made her more determined to keep him at arm's length.

Sally sat at a table on the drinks deck. She was feeling sick. She tried to read but the relentless throbbing of the engines echoed in her stomach and the type was dancing in front of her eyes. It really was a hellish way to travel. A bottle of duty-free Glenfiddich sat in front of her, splendid in its wax-sealed box.

Harry was bored. He had circled the ship twice in search of diversion. He had tried to strike up a conversation with some of the football supporters clustered round the space invader machines but one of them had spotted his gay badge. His attempt at comradely banter, usually so easily taken up, was greeted with ribald derision.

He sat opposite Sally now, shifting restlessly from one buttock to the other, willing her to look up from her book and talk. She stoically ignored him. He looked around for some diversion, but there was none. He tried the direct approach.

'So tell me Sally, what will you be doing at this conference?' he asked.

She lowered the book momentarily. Considered the question. 'Well, we'll talk. Exchange ideas and experiences. Get to know a bit more about each other's problems . . .'

'A bit like what we've being doing?'

She allowed him a cross between a frosty smile and an all-out lip curl. 'Well, with a bit of luck the conversation might soar to even greater heights than we've aspired to.'

His lower jaw dropped slightly. Well, this was no holds barred and so sweetly put. He decided to let it go and carry on in conversational mode.

'But still. Look at us. We're different and yet we've got things in common . . .'

She lowered the book more decidedly this time. 'Such as . . .?'

'Well . . .' He cast about. They had very little in common that he could see. His eyes settled on the bottle. 'Well, we both like Glenfiddich . . .'

'Hey, yeah. So we do! Well, that's it then. Let's get engaged.' She brandished the book at him. 'Look, I'm *trying* to read a book. What do you want me to do? Take out adoption papers?'

This was too much for Harry's dignity. He got to his feet. 'Okay. I was only trying to make a bit of human contact.' He moved off a few paces then turned back, aggrieved. 'You know, even dogs stop and sniff one another,' he said and he stalked off, slinging his jacket over his shoulder with the air of someone who'd delivered a trump card.

His victory began to feel a little hollow as he took his fourth turn past the football supporters. They were now paralytically drunk and chanting, 'Liverpool, Liverpool, Liverpool.' One of their number was standing on the bar, trying to shin up the steel strut while three Belgian bar stewards tried to peel him off by his trousers. The brothers were moving in for support and it looked like a free-for-all any moment. His resentment against her began to ebb. After all, he was here. She had done him an enormous favour. It was his duty to make it as painless as possible for her. She was a bit scratchy, she obviously didn't like him but then, why should she?

In her turn, Sally, having insisted on her privacy and the right to read her book, had now lost total interest in it. She had asserted herself. So what? She was now reliving the unpleasant little spat in a loop which prevented the words on the page entering her busied brain. She felt rather churlish. He'd only tried to make a little light conversation. On impulse, she went to the bar and got two glasses.

He came back looking rather shamefaced, bearing a packet of Marzine and a tumbler full of water.

'Oh, that's very thought . . .' she began, then stopped as he put a bottle of Chanel down in front of her with some show of diffidence. She blinked at it. He realised too late it was all wrong. It smacked of courtship, as if he'd got the Travellers column mixed up with the Lonely Hearts. And didn't feminists eschew perfume?

'Thank you. There was no need . . .' she began, the colour rising.

'Oh, I'm so stupid. You probably don't wear perfume,' he said, hitting his head at the blunder.

'I do. Yes I do, sometimes.' She opened the box gingerly as if it might contain a tropical spider. 'For myself.'

'Well of course for yourself,' he said. 'No point putting it on for anyone else if you don't like men.'

She realised, not for the first time since her foot had first touched the gas pedal on this misconceived adventure, that his grasp of feminism was unformed and dimly gleaned from the *Daily Mirror*. She saw no point in trying to set him right. 'Do you want to crack open the malt?' she asked.

They smiled at one another. In the smile was a tacit acceptance

44

that they were stuck with one another and they would both try to be nice.

They rolled off the ferry at around four o'clock. Belgium was sunny and, with the cobbled streets and the trams and driving on the right, it seemed very foreign to Harry. He had difficulty in concealing his genuine excitement. He sat forward in his seat and craned up at the gothic buildings.

'To think they got this far,' he said. 'To think they got this close.'

'Who?' she asked and then, 'Oh, the Germans?' She looked around her vaguely. 'Does it make a difference seeing it?'

He nodded intensely. She supposed it did. She tried to imagine a world picture as limited as Harry's and she failed. She had been brought up in Kenya and spent some of her childhood in India and Dubai.

'But it's a bit late now, isn't it? I mean, we're trying to bury it.'

She was talking to the air.

Each road sign they passed meant something to him in terms of the second-hand folk history of his family, and she could tell that the Second World War was the only chance of justified heroism the Hammels had ever had. And if the boundaries of his world were indeed the boundaries of a tabloid newspaper, she could only say thank God it was turning out to be the *Mirror* and not the *Sun*.

As night fell, the German customs post came up quite unexpectedly in the darkness as a line of flashing, adrenalising lights strung across a broad highway, steeply banked with the menacing silhouette of a forest. No sooner had Harry seen the sign ahead than he began to rummage feverishly in the back like a badger digging into a sett.

'What are you doing?' she asked. German customs was just a formality but any show of furtiveness was bound to put them on their mettle. 'For God's sake, be normal.'

'My mate went through Checkpoint Charlie,' he said. 'They impounded his cassettes, spent two hours listening to his head cleaner.' He stuffed them under a jumper.

A car was being unpacked by the roadside. A swarthy man, maybe an arab, was explaining something to the impassive guards. The television was being taken down off the roof rack, and Sally felt the chill in the atmosphere. It was something to do with the gun holsters, the steely faces of the officers, the fact that a sniffer dog was standing by, eyes bright and alert.

Harry handed across the passports, in a cold sweat. He looked from the steel-rimmed glasses to the pebble eyes. The officer returned his gaze with cool penetration, assessing Harry's terrorist potential. Then his eyes moved to Sally and he gave her a broad wink and pursed his lips into a small moue. Harry was taken aback by this mimed interchange. If Sally had for a few moments suspected him of being a drug courier, he was now turning over the suspicion that he might be travelling with someone from an intelligence agency. How else would they have cleared so smoothly?

' 'Ere,' he said after a while. 'Was your father in the Foreign Office?'

'No, he's in a communications firm,' she said. Harry grunted, as though this was extremely significant. She tried to puzzle out why he'd asked but it was a little too much for her tired brain. When he offered, she let him take over the driving.

Chapter 5

Around eleven thirty his eyes were beginning to sting and he had trouble keeping his concentration. There had been few gasthauses on the way and he was worried that they might not find another one on this deserted road. Then, as they turned the corner, he saw to his relief a large rambling mansion in extensive grounds with a hotel sign. He pulled into the empty car park. Sally was fast asleep beside him, the map spread out limply in her hand. He had decided to navigate the last twenty miles without waking her and it had given him a crick in his neck craning to see the A-roads on her knee.

He looked at her face now as she slept. He hesitated to break the spell. She had the placid, untroubled vulnerability of a five-year-old but he knew, once he woke her, she would snap into another person, touchy and brittle.

'This do you, princess?'

She stirred. She became dimly aware that there was a coat over her and he'd stuffed something behind her head for a pillow. Again she was touched. They were curiously intimate attentions that he paid her.

'Where are we?' she asked feebly, still half in a dream.

'I don't know,' he said with a shrug. 'You're the one with the map.'

She stumbled out dopily into the cool night air. There were lights on in the house, far back in the empty bar.

'You go in,' said Harry, 'I'll just start setting up camp.'

He pulled the tent out of the back. She hesitated.

'You know, I wouldn't have put you down as the outdoors type,' she said. The grounds looked bleak and inhospitable.

'Me? Yeah. Love it,' he said.

47

'Do you think it's allowed?' she asked. 'I mean, shouldn't you ask someone?' She thought it was a very odd thing to want to do after a long day's driving.

'Oh, you can camp anywhere in Europe,' he said airily. He had a vague idea that this was true. Anyway, he was past caring. He was exhausted and he just wanted to get the whole depressing palaver over with. He dragged out the sleeping bag.

Sally wandered off with her valise. The room was furnished barely but it was comfortable and cheap. She hung up a few silk shirts, opened the mini-fridge and poured herself a glass of wine. She wanted to check over her notes. Maybe make some amendments on the pocket recorder. She read through the manuscript. It wasn't a world-shattering piece of prose. It broke no new ground but at least, she told herself, it was all her own, gropingly arrived at through painful experience, fitting together pieces of jigsaw, comparing notes with other women, happening upon books that seemed suddenly to illuminate one whole area of her life and make sense of it.

> As if a woman quietly walked away
> From the argument and jargon
> in a room
> And sitting down in the kitchen
> turning in her lap
> Bits of yarn, calico and velvet
> scraps . . .

She mused on the Adrienne Rich poem she had used to preface the first section. That was how it was, piecing together seemingly unconnected scraps into a picture of the world where women represented a vast pool of impotence, their talents squandered, their perceptions unregarded as emotional and unsound. She began to speak into the dictaphone.

'While women continue to see themselves as inactive partners emotionally supporting men, this continues to *appear* to be the true role given them by nature: natural because it's customary, custom-

48

ary because it's convenient to those who are emotionally supported . . .'

As she paced past the window she became aware of Harry, a small figure in the garden below her, flailing ineffectually with the fabric of his tent.

'Radical feminism posits separatism as the only true and valid response to a situation . . .' His head was enveloped now in billowing nylon and he was vainly attempting to stab the vertical support into the soft ground. She switched off the machine.

'Do you want any help?' she called down.

He paused, squinted up at the window, located her face. 'No thanks,' he said, with a cheerfulness he did not feel. 'It's all part of the fun, putting it up.'

He saw her flit away from the window and turned dejectedly to the task in hand. It looked so simple and yet there must be some vital stage he had overlooked, because the thing just wouldn't go up. The ground sheet was pegged, the guy ropes seemed to be in all the places guy ropes should be but without the instruction book it was hard to check. There seemed nowhere at all to put the vertical strut, which was far too short to support the structure anyway.

'Are you sure you don't need any help?'

He crawled out and she was looming over him with a miniature bottle of whisky in her hand.

'Thanks. Thanks a lot,' he said.

She took the mallet out of his hand and walked round the tent, assessing the situation. She repositioned one or two of the metal skewers and bashed them in firmly.

'I hate camping,' she said. 'It's one of those things. I can't see any lure to the great outdoors. And I hate spiders.' She began to dismantle his handiwork. He was using the ridge pole for a vertical.

'We had great times when we were kids,' he said nostalgically, 'you know, flames flickering on the faces of the seventh Kirby scout troop. Following the track of a three-legged badger. Filling the smoky air with our young voices . . .'

49

He began to sing in a low reverent voice:
'Ging gang gooly gooly gooly gooly watcha,
Ging gang goo, ging gang goo
Ging gang gooly gooly gooly gooly watcha
Ging gang goo, ging gang goo . . .'
He watched her methodically straightening out the fabric.
'Good words, aren't they? Were you a guide?'

She frowned. 'I was a brownie.' She thought back. Saw herself in her little brown pixie outfit, solemnly stuffing woollen bunny rabbits with second-hand kapok to send to the poor black babies starving in Africa. Her brother had gone off to camp to do arctic rolls in a kayak.

'While you were swinging intrepidly from trees, I was up to my elbows in sour nappies working for the scrubbing badge.' She wondered how he had managed to get the whole structure inverted and all the flaps inside out.

'Still, when you're a kid, you don't care, do you?' He wished he hadn't got on to the subject.

'I also spent a lot of time running round a wooden toadstool flapping my wings,' she said shortly as she pulled the end rope tight and got the structure on its feet.

'Doesn't seem to have done them any harm. They're still there on your back sprinkling fairy dust and good deeds. Here you are lending me a hand . . .'

She stood up, worried. There was something missing. 'If you want my opinion,' she said as she turned the accessory bag out, looking for the missing section of the upright, 'the scout movement's reactionary and imperialistic and it forces the worst possible sexual stereotypes on young children.'

'Oh,' he said. He didn't really want her opinion, and if a simple interchange on scouting produced a political tract, he wondered what other minefields he'd managed to scrape through without setting off a device. 'I only went for the cakes at teatime.'

She was grovelling around under the bush now trying to see if the thing could have rolled. 'I *made* the cakes at teatime,' came the muffled retort.

Harry attempted a joke. 'Well, I can see you didn't get much practice with the tents.'

The thing was flapping ineffectually, unsupported. She looked up at him murderously. Her eyes lit on his hip pocket, where the upright section was glinting. She drew it out with silent accusation and fitted it. The tent stood upright, satisfactorily assembled.

'You know, this thing's not really meant for outdoors,' she said, looking at it sorrowfully. 'It's only one up from a wendy house.'

Harry scowled, affronted. He had got it reduced in the sale because of a slight flaw in the fabric. He was not relishing a night out under the stars and it was turning rather blowy. If he could have afforded a better tent then he could have afforded to stay in a civilised hotel bed like anyone else. This much, he thought savagely, was pretty bloody obvious.

'Okay. Look. You've been a lot of help. I can manage the flap door meself.'

She stood up. The thing was as secure as it could ever be, considering its flimsiness. She doubted the wisdom of putting it under a tree, but still.

Harry tried to remain civil while at the same time getting rid of her. 'You go and get in the warm,' he assured her. 'I'm great. You don't want to be out here getting chilled to the bone.'

'Okay. Goodnight,' she said. She plodded back towards the house. He watched her slouching towards her central heating, probably a duckdown duvet and a soft, plump pillow. He raised his voice marginally at her retreating back: 'I was only in two weeks anyway. They threw me out because we couldn't afford the uniform.'

She half-heard him, frowned and carried on.

'I bet you had a uniform all right,' he muttered darkly.

She tried to finish her amendments, but almost as soon as her head touched the pillow, a warm, drowsy feeling of well-being came over her and the dictaphone continued to hiss in her limp hand.

She heard the first rumble of thunder but managed to accommodate it convincingly in her dream. Harry was dressed as Charles the Second and he was driving her to park the jeep in a multi-storey car park with a lift. But as they drove into the elevator, she knew it just wasn't there and they plunged down the lift shaft for an eternity. Falling, falling in slow motion, waiting for the impact. As the car richocheted off the shaft wall, it boomed and echoed.

It was the worst storm in three years. The rain bucketed down in the depression of the valley where the hotel stood. Lightning pencilled jaggedly across the sky then opened out like a firework and the thunder boomed as though the angels were shaking a giant steel sheet. The tree Harry had selected for its shelter gathered the water, then poured it down more gently but in concentrated quantities on the tent below.

Harry stirred to find that it was not a stout tattooed wrestler kneeling on his stomach as he had half-thought in his twilight sleep but a great weight of freezing water bowing down the nylon canopy and threatening to cling-wrap him like an orange mummy.

In his sleep-fuddled state he had a vague sense of danger, as though the collapsed structure might suck to his face like a polythene bag. He squirmed himself around and poked his head out. A cold sluice of water tipped from its gully and doused his scalp. He recoiled, gasping with the icy shock. The sudden movement bowed the upright inwards and brought it down with a smart tap on his head. Mumbling furiously, he crawled out of the tent. He wriggled free of the bag and stood up, taking the full torrent of the teeming rain, staring blankly at the deflated hulk. He made a few half-hearted attempts to right it but things were too far gone. The end guy pegs had pulled away from the sopping mud and one had been swept away in the little stream that eddied past the tent flap. It was nowhere to be seen. The rain ran in rivulets down Harry's neck, beat a noisy tattoo on his raincoat and trickled in copious runnels round his bare legs. He rallied. Weights. He needed weights.

He cast around wildly until his eyes lit on the immaculate

rockery. It shone like a dim fairy grotto under the coloured light bulbs. There was a hive of worker gnomes going about their business amongst the lichens and mosses. He darted across and chose some hefty ones, skeetered back, plonked two firmly either end and attached the guy ropes round their necks. He straightened up, satisfied. Now the thing was anchored but it needed something more drastic to get it buoyant. He eyed the tree branch overhead. It looked good and solid. What was called for was a primitive shaduf structure using the branch as a fulcrum.

He bent down and scrambled frantically into the tent, emerging backwards with the coil of rope and his sailor's duffel bag. With an inspired sense of purpose, he began to bunch the loose, wet fabric of the tent top into a cluster and wound the rope around it in a knot. He tied a concrete gnome to the other end of the rope as ballast, then took aim. He slung it with all his might at the pale moon that peered wanly through the bristling leaves. The rope looped up in a perfect arc and caught the branch so that the gnome dangled, swinging, just in reach. He hauled it down and the tent drew itself up correspondingly to a flattened pyramid. He was drenched to the skin now, so the exercise was becoming academic, but he applied himself with the dogged frenzy of someone who's started something and intends to see it through.

He ran repeated trips from the tent to the rockery, ferrying gnomes and rocks, churning the mud underfoot into a hazardous slurry. Slipping and sliding this way and that, he stuffed the duffel bag to bursting point then attached it to the rope and let the dead weight winch the tent up. It was almost there. He slithered back to muster the last few conscripts, stuck them in his pockets, staggered back, tore off the raincoat and shrouded it round the duffel bag. The rope plummeted that extra foot and hauled the tent up into an upright position. Harry shot his arms up in the air, elated. Success. A perfect balancing act.

He turned to crawl back in, flushed with success. As he did so, his eyes fell on the sleeping bag, lying where he'd peeled it off – in a large, growing puddle of rainwater, completely soaked through. Wearily he got to his feet. He was filled with a sudden rage after all his efforts – he gave it a flying kick across the garden, then followed through, picked it up and hurled it with all his energy into the duck pond. It slapped across a wooden creosoted box and a great honking and quacking started up as seven or eight indignant ducks began to flurry out in a squawking mass of alarm. It was at this point that he became dimly aware of a red and blue light winking powerfully on the road above. Two dots of light were weaving cautiously towards him through the trees. He stared mesmerised at the will o' the wisps as they wavered and hovered, seeming magically to glow and expand. Then they came into focus. Two rubber torches followed by two men in khaki uniforms and peaked caps approached him out of the darkness, their faces set like hatchets, their hands on their revolvers, one of them clinging to the leash of a red-eyed wolf.

It was the sound of the siren that woke her, its piercing wail penetrating her dream-sleep until she could deny its reality no longer. She jolted into consciousness. She imagined she heard some gruff altercation in German, the sound of a car door. The flasher unit bounced red and blue light across the far wall. She ran to the window. The car was pulling out on the road that wound up above the hotel. She looked down anxiously to the spot where Harry had pitched his tent. Her blood froze. There, under the muted fairy lights of the ornamental garden, she could see Harry's limp form, shrouded in his raincoat, swinging eerily from an improvised noose. A crack of lightning poured white-blue light on the creaking bough as it groaned with its sombre burden.

All the colour drained from her face, her eyes wide with horror. She ran down the stairs four at a time, like some demented dervish, swerving round the bannisters and out of the hotel, through the driving rain, barefoot through the soaking marsh of ruined turf towards the place where his body hung. If only she had made an effort to know him perhaps she might have prevented . . . but then . . . Maybe there was still a chance he was alive – one heard of cases where people lived . . . and there again, how could she have prevented it, she hardly knew him. Where had the police car gone? For help? For an ambulance? As she ran closer, a million disparate thoughts jumbled through her brain, all focused on the strange misshapen lump that was Harry's face – a strange, horrific, garish mixture of colours, almost as though it had been gloss-painted red and green and pink . . . It was only then that the image cohered. It was not Harry's face at all but a large benign gnome from the demolished rockery, poking through the top button of the raincoat and grinning at its broken fishing rod.

She stood and let the emotions drain out of her, feeling very foolish and very angry and flooded with overwhelming relief. She looked around for clues. Someone had systematically dismantled the rockery. A few of the punier gnomes lay where he had discarded them, their noses in the slime. Caches of pebbles were scattered about like the hoard of some manic rodent. His sleeping bag had been sucked into the mechanism of the fountain. What little water was managing to circulate spurted up chunks of sponge from the stuffing. The ducks were huddled mournfully in the débris. There was no sign of Harry himself and she was fairly certain he would be languishing in a very small hard cell with a hostile constabulary. Good, she thought maliciously. And they can keep him as long as they like 'cos I'm not getting him out.

Rather mechanically, she levered herself into the jeep. She still had on her nightshirt but it could pass off as a dress. It was dripping wet and her hair was plastered to her face in limp whorls. She set off in the direction the police car had taken. Let's see you get out of this one, she thought savagely as she swerved to avoid a small wet rabbit, let's see you try out your charm on the German police.

But as the rain subsided to a fine blue mizzle in the half-light, the depressing truth dawned. Actually the West German police force didn't have that good a reputation. Angharad's brother had been held for four days on a tenuous charge and got a crack across the head that left his hearing impaired. That, of course, had been a case where they vaguely suspected him of terrorist contacts. But what were they holding Harry for? It was a comfort he could speak the language. She didn't envy him any. She wasn't very keen on the Notting Hill police and these ones had much more lethal-looking truncheons *and* they carried pistols. If Harry really hit a problem, they were some way from an embassy. And then how long might they hold him? Two days, three days? She hoped he was all right.

She found the police station a few miles on the far outskirts of town. The desk sergeant led her through. It was a long, antiseptic corridor with garishly bright neons. It led to an open-barred iron door, which he opened with ponderous self-importance. He pulled it behind them with a final ominous clang and locked it. The doors along the route had metal viewing shutters. She realised there were probably some sad little stories penned in behind the doors. The smell of disinfectant grew more pungent as they paced onwards. Somewhere, in the bowels of the cell-block, there was a gathering of some sort. She could hear gales of relaxed laughter.

It seemed to be inappropriate and wrong somehow to be laughing in this place where the petty tragedies of people's lives were spattered behind the blandly spotless walls. Harry, lying in a tiny inhospitable cell without his shoelaces. For God's sake, all he'd done was pitch his tent in someone's ornamental garden. The laughter erupted again and grew louder. It sounded as though someone was hysterically choking on a biscuit. The officer turned off into a smoke-filled room.

Harry sat in the corner, wrapped in a blanket, a steaming mug of coffee in front of him and a big sandwich in his hand, holding forth to a relaxed bunch of affable-looking policemen. Harry was just remembering a new joke as the laughter was tailing off from the last.

'Two Irish policemen.'

The two officers who were translating conferred.

'Irländer.'

'Okay, two Irländer policemen in a patrol car. One says 'ere, I don't think the flashing light's working. The other says stop the car and I'll have a look. So he gets out and the first cop says well, is it working? And the other one says . . .' Harry wobbled his head dumbly from side to side. 'Yes. No. Yes. No. Yes. No.'

The two who understood English started to fall about laughing again.

'*Ja, nein, ja, nein, ja, nein* . . .'

Sally stood in the doorway, her face set hard, viewing the scene of disordered hilarity. Her focus shifted to the sandwich in Harry's hand. The Germans were conferring now over the translation of a gem from their repertoire. Harry felt someone's eyes boring into him and looked up.

'Hey,' he said as if greeting new arrivals at a particularly loose and laid-back party. 'Sally. Look this is Sally. The girl I told you about.'

'Ah.' They all nodded gravely, appraising her.

'She's a great girl.'

Sally continued to stare transfixed at his right hand. 'What's that you're eating?'

He quailed under her eye, looked guilty at the sausage obscenely overhanging the coarse brown bread.

'Er, that.' He looked evasively at it as though it had settled in his hand when he wasn't looking. 'Well, it's a sandwich.'

'What kind of sandwich?' she pursued.

'It's very nice. I didn't think to look what was in it.'

'It's a sausage sandwich,' she said firmly. She turned on her heel and began to walk down the corridor.

'Think I'd better be going now, if that's all right,' he said with a small look skywards and a waggle of the fingers to indicate to them trouble on the horizon. They nodded. Trouble with the little woman was something they all understood.

She waited at the gate. He hopped behind her in his underpants and socks, holding his shoes. The officer let them through.

'Well, maybe it *was* a sausage,' he said, 'I don't know, it didn't taste like a sausage. Not like an English one anyway.'

They walked out into the bleak dawn across the car park, Harry trying to keep pace.

'Vegetarians don't eat sausages,' she said coldly.

'People do all sorts of things in situations of stress,' he answered to her uncompromising back. 'They *have* been known to eat one another.'

She swung into the jeep and started the engine.

'It was a sausage, you know. Not a human leg.'

They drove along in silence. Sally white and drawn, stuck in a mental warp somewhere between exhaustion and fury, Harry unrepentant and flushed with righteous indignation.

In the cold early morning light, the damage to the ornamental garden was revealed in its full enormity. The hotelier was waiting for them, a small, grim blonde woman rather like a pekingese but with an alsatian's vocal chords. She had a long plait slung over her shoulder and wore a substantial dressing gown. She stood above them on the patio above the rockery, policing them with folded arms as they half-heartedly attempted to reposition the rocks and the chipped gnomes, under her stern and incomprehensible directions. Harry's lilo blew forlornly round the ruined turf like a balloon after a disappointing party. The woman kept up a continuous harangue as they laboured below her like a pair of unhappy convicts.

Harry listlessly held up one of the bambis for Sally's advice. 'I don't suppose you remember where this little fella went?'

'Ask her,' said Sally shortly.

Harry hesitated. The woman was glowering dourly at him. 'Er . . . *Wer geht diese knome?*'

She pointed gravely to its former position behind the wishing well.

'*Wir werden Sie für den Schaden am Brunnen verantwortlich machen,*' she said decisively. '*Die pumpe ist voller Federn.*'

'What's she saying?' asked Sally.

Harry shook his head. 'I didn't catch it that time.'

'*Sie müssen den gesamten Schaden bezahlen und dann möchte ich Sie hier nie wieder sehen. Ansonsten kommt Mein Mann mit dem Gewehr.*'

She smiled unpleasantly at them. Sally waited expectantly for Harry to translate.

'Well?'

'I think she's softening a bit.'

58

'. . . *und glauben Sie nicht, dass er nur Spass macht!*'

He checked Sally before she could press him further. 'Hold on, it's a very unusual dialect . . .'

He walked up the steps to bring himself level with the woman, his ear slightly cocked as she delivered another machine-gun burst. He stooped as though fine-tuning his ear to the nuance of her regional speech. She was smiling cordially. 'See, yes. She's smiling . . . I think she's saying we can have breakfast after all.'

Harry and Sally both smiled and nodded obsequiously at her.

'*Frühstuck fur zwei?*' he asked tentatively.

The woman, goaded beyond bearing, pinioned him roughly in an armlock and hauled him up the remaining steps, then frog-marched him off along the path.

Once inside, the woman, seeing Harry quiescent and subdued, released her grip. She slid open the door of the store cupboard and indicated its contents. Harry peered in. He could see Sally's suitcases in the gloom. The woman slid the door closed, locked it firmly and dangled the keys at her bosom so that her intentions were clear to him.

Sally hovered uncertainly, some distance away at the door. He mooched over to her, unsure how to convey the new information.

'Ah, little hiccough in the translating there.' He avoided her eye. 'No breakfast and she's holding your luggage hostage.'

Sally peered at him. Was she really hearing what she thought she was hearing?

'Ask her if she'll take sterling travellers cheques.' She threw it out like a challenge.

He half-opened his mouth to begin a feeble excuse.

'You can't, can you? You don't speak German, do you?'

He shut his mouth unhappily. She pulled out her travellers cheques furiously and slammed the wallet down on the counter. The woman wrote down an astronomical figure. Sally began to sign mechanically, tossing each page over, gathering momentum until she had signed half the book. Harry watched uneasily.

'I'll pay you back, Sally,' he ventured in an undertone. 'Honest I will.'

'Get the luggage,' she said.

They drove in silence. It was autobahn mostly with urban squalor sandwiched in between the long, dull stretches.

'I don't know why you're making such a big thing about it,' he said mutinously. 'You can't speak it either.'

'I never pretended I could,' she pointed out.

'How come you missed out on it then?'

'I did Spanish and French,' she said shortly.

'Yes, well I did woodwork and remedials.'

'Remedials for what?'

'I had slightly knock knees, if you must know,' he said reluctantly.

'And that took up your entire school career?'

'Yes, well, they gave up on the brain quite early but they persevered with the knees.'

'What about religious knowledge? You know, telling lies and going to hell and all that.'

He sat up, stung by the accusation. 'I didn't lie. I said I'd been *learnin'* it.' He began to rummage in his cassette box to back up his point. 'I've done one side of the tape . . .'

He slotted it in. The sound of a hospitable bar faded up, cash registered clinking, a low babble of conversation and draught pumps being pulled. A stilted woman's voice intervened.

'You have now reached the bar and you want to order.'

'*Was möchten Sie trinken?*' the barman enquired cordially.

Harry inserted his answer in the silence. '*Ich möchte ein gross bier bitte.*' He looked at her for approval. 'That means I'd like a big one, please,' he confided. 'Side one was social interchange and side two was airports. There wasn't anything on prisons.'

'No, I suppose not,' she said, distantly.

'Look.' He felt oddly depressed. He liked her. He wanted her to like him. And yet the situation he'd manoeuvred for himself meant he would always be in the wrong at every turn. 'I'm sorry, Sally.

I'm sorry if I've not come up to scratch.' He trailed off, inadequately. He thought about explaining things. Would she understand? Her face was set like a muzzle. No.

She stated the facts baldly.

'You said you'd been learning German. You didn't say you were halfway through your first tape.'

'I never said I was fluent. Anyway, you wouldn't have brought me if you'd known, would you?'

'No,' she said energetically, 'I bloody well wouldn't.'

'Well, there you are.' He sat back with the pained air of someone who has successfully defended a case. 'I've got enough disadvantages without telling people things they don't ask.'

She was about to point out that this was not a simple sin of omission when she realised it was a complete waste of breath. He understood all right. 'You're impossible!' she hissed through clenched teeth.

'I may be impossible,' he said with a small gleam of satisfaction, 'but I'm *here*.'

You are for the moment, she thought darkly, but don't get yourself too settled. They were too far off the beaten track for her to pack him off here and now but, come the next big town . . . I'll give you till – she scanned the map – Rüdesheim.

They stopped for lunch at a service station. Sally read her book stoically. Harry declined to eat but sat, facing away from her, looking moodily into the far distance. He was turning over a problem in his mind. He had hardly any money left. He could do one more tank of petrol and then that was it. Somehow he had imagined petrol to be very cheap on the continent. Of course, there'd been something of a shortfall on the travelling expenses even before he'd left. He'd convinced himself that something would turn up.

Sally shrugged off his attempt to take the next shift of driving. The less she involved him, the easier it would be to off-load him. She opted for a B-road to vary the monotony of the autobahn. Harry curled up and tried to sleep. He wedged his head between the seat rest and the roof strut and let his face smear against the plastic window. The vibrations went through his head like a dentist's drill. Money. Everything in this world came down to money. In his case, the lack of it.

The high perimeter fence of a US Air Force base strobed bleakly by for an eternity, its drabness broken only by glimpses of camouflaged bombers lined up like obedient schnauzers. He closed his eyes. He could see no alternative. When they reached the next big town, he'd have to do the decent thing and split.

He was obviously ruining her enjoyment. She certainly wasn't adding to his, and he could hardly expect someone to subsidise him, even temporarily, when they found it a struggle to so much as look him in the eyes. She had the radio on to discourage conversation, the American Forces Network. A fatherly voice was warning the boys to stay off marijuana because it might affect their performance in the cockpit. An F-111 screamed overhead. It was impossible to sleep. Sighing, he pulled out a copy of *Weekend* that he'd found on a ferry seat and flicked through it in a desultory fashion until he lit upon a competition. The radio kept cutting out in a maddening way and was punctuated with blasts of white noise. Sally fiddled with it, a puzzled frown on her face.

'I wonder why it keeps doing that?' she muttered.

'Maybe they're jamming it,' he said, working on a vague prompting that she would respond to a conspiracy theory. She ran it through the waveband. 'On the other hand, you may have fixed the wires wrong.'

The fact that she'd broken the silence encouraged him to speak.

'Look, I've got to put these dogs in order of appeal. Which do you prefer? The winsome terrier or the pug with a bent ear? There's a car in it for me and a year's supply of dog food for you.'

She didn't smile.

'I'm stuck on the apt and witty phrase.'

She allowed her eye to rest unwillingly on the dog portraits. 'How about "jellied horse meat makes my dog sick and so do your puerile advertising methods"?'

He counted the words off thoughtfully on his fingers, to see if they fitted.

'It's got a ring to it,' he conceded. 'Still, wouldn't mind the car, though, would you?' And then, as an afterthought, 'How much did this thing cost you?'

'About fifteen hundred.'

Harry's jaw dropped open. He almost spluttered.

'But you could have got something decent . . .' He corrected himself, too late. 'I mean something ready-made-up!'

He had never spent more than two hundred on any one of his succession of troubled Cortinas. The last one had been so battered that someone took it to be a wreck and stole the wheels.

Sally drew breath, testily. 'But that wasn't the point, was it?'

Harry nodded. 'No.' He thought about it. 'Er . . . what was the point, then? I've forgotten.'

'Just bloody well doing it,' she said. 'It was an aim.'

Harry looked unimpressed. How luxurious it must be to have the money to finance every passing whim. To think, why, let's build a car, and nothing to stop you from doing it. He thought of all the ways a person could spend fifteen hundred pounds. The knowledge that they would part company soon freed him to speak his mind.

'My idea of an aim is to have so much money I never have to look inside an engine ever again. Spend a little time in a car factory and the whole thing loses its mystique. You're fighting for the right to do what I'm fighting for the right *not* to do. Strange, isn't it?'

She was reluctant to engage. 'You're confusing two different issues,' she said calmly. 'Making this car was about *personal* development. You're talking about exploitation when you talk about car works.'

Harry folded his arms stubbornly. 'I'm saying, I can't see why you want to muck about with cars when you don't have to.'

She approached Harry now with the same dutiful weariness she felt when tackling racist London cab-drivers.

'There's a lot of factors militating against women. Start with the obvious ones. Lack of mobility. Ignorance of technology. Those things deprive women of any sort of choice in the way they run their lives.'

63

'Oh yeah?' Harry snorted. 'My sister's got a car. She uses it to drive to and from the canning factory. Helps her get the dinner ready quicker. I wouldn't say it contributed to her emancipation. I'd say it made her a more cost-effective machine.'

Sally let out an irritated sigh. 'Well, exactly, who's arguing? But we're talking about two different problems. Why is she *having* to run a home and work in a factory?'

It seemed so glaringly obvious to her.

Harry struggled to remember what choices he or his sister had made. He didn't actually remember there being much choice. 'Well,' he ventured, 'it was quite near and she wasn't very brainy.' He tried a winning smile.

She stared at him incredulously for a moment, then shook her head with pitying contempt. 'You don't have any political awareness at all, do you?'

Harry looked moodily down at his paper.

'Look,' she said, trying one last stab. 'The capitalist system is predicated on exploitation of labour, right?'

He continued to stare sullenly at the dogs.

'The labour force functions because of the unpaid domestic labour of women, right? So if you want change, where do you start to politicise?'

He eyed her insolently, then picked up his biro. 'I thought the pug was more appealing,' he said, and began to fill in the boxes with spider figures.

She coloured with anger. 'Yeah,' she said, 'you go back to your appealing dogs. I always wondered what sort of morons those things were aimed at. Now I know.'

Harry's face darkened perceptibly. 'Moron. Right. Okay,' he said coldly, 'well, I know my place.'

She immediately regretted it. 'Look, I didn't mean you were a moron, it's just, well, we're talking on different levels.'

'Yes. You're talking on a high level and I'm talking on a low level. The more things change, the more they stay the same.'

'Hey Harry,' she protested. She could see he was mortally offended.

'Let's leave it alone, shall we?' he said sullenly. 'You just drive and I'll just read the map. We won't attempt any more class analyses.'

'It wasn't a class analysis . . .' She saw that his jaw was set in a stubborn line and she would get nowhere placating him. 'Oh, if you're going to sulk . . .'

'No, it was probably a personal analysis. Your personal analysis of me is that I'm a moron. My personal analysis of you is that you're a bitch. Shall we leave it there?'

She was startled at his vehemence. There seemed nothing much to say. 'Oh. Right.' She fixed her eyes firmly on the road ahead and prepared for another long stretch of siege.

Apart from terse directions from Harry, they didn't speak again until late afternoon. She had an uneasy feeling that they'd missed some vital signpost. There had been nothing for a good half-hour. They came to a four-way intersection. She dithered. She wasn't prepared to swallow her pride and ask for a decision and he proffered none. She swung right. Harry jolted awake. He had just begun to slip away for a moment.

'Where are you going?' he asked.

'This should bring us back to the autobahn,' she said. 'There ought to be a slip road in a few hundred metres.'

'Are you sure about that?' was all he said.

'Yes.' She wasn't but the alternative was to double back meekly. And, logically, she told herself, this *ought* to be the road to take. But as they put more miles behind them she had a sinking feeling that all was not right. The scenery was flattening out into even bleaker scrub land and the road surface was becoming more pitted and uneven, peppering the windshield with sudden showers of gravel, coming at them like shot-blast. It was beginning to look more like some Godforsaken piece of American folk history than West Germany. There were no signposts and there were no clues and Harry was maintaining an infuriating, impassive silence.

Then she saw a garage, standing isolated, like a mirage, some way off on a dust road. It stood in front of a fenced scrap-metal compound. At first she took it to be an abandoned shell but then she saw the jeeps lined up at the diesel pump. She pulled up in the forecourt, in front of a cream thirties building with a stained and peeling facade. Now she was closer, she could see that it had a modern extension with a lurid neon sign: CLUB FLAMINGO SAUNA AND MASSAGE PARLOUR.

She began to fill up the jeep. The soldiers watched her.

'Is it far to get back on the autobahn?' she called.

One of them ambled closer. He ran his eye over her body with practised insouciance. 'What's your hurry?' he drawled, addressing his answer pointedly to her chest.

Harry's chivalrous impulses were at a low ebb but he levered himself heavily out of the jeep and sauntered over to stand beside her, protectively. There were some GIs going into the club with their arms around two little Filipino girls. Somehow this place offended his proprieties in a way that strip joints in London never had.

'You'd think they owned the place, wouldn't you?' he muttered.

The soldier weighed Harry up. Sally felt near to tears. They were hopelessly lost. It would be nightfall before they reached Rüdesheim. All she wanted was a warm bath and a cold glass of wine and here she was on a dirt track beside a brothel waiting for Harry to pick a fight with two soldiers built like tanks.

'It's all right,' she said. 'Don't feel you have to be macho. I can cope.'

Harry reddened slightly. This was the last time he'd do her any favours. But he stood his ground. 'So, where's the autobahn from here, mate?' he asked.

'You're way off,' said the GI, losing interest now he was facing a couple. 'I guess you'd best head on back the way you came.'

Harry turned and stalked back to the jeep. He got into the driving seat. Tapped the steering wheel and pretended to whistle unconcernedly while she settled the payment. When she thumped in beside him he was already gunning the engine and they screeched off with a burning of tyres in the direction from which they'd come. It took an eternity to get back to the original intersection. She looked at her watch. It was already nine o'clock.

She was aware that Harry was emanating a black wall of hostility that was almost tangible.

'Which way?' he demanded.

'Right.' He swung right so violently that they both lurched like pendulums.

'Where now?'

They were doing seventy and the lines on the map danced in front of her eyes like so many meaningless coloured worms.

'Another right, I think.' She stabbed the map ineffectually. 'This is where we want to go – Boppard.'

'There's no point stabbing the map and expecting me to drive to where you've stabbed,' he said drily. 'You're supposed to navigate.'

'*Left!*' she shouted. He had begun the manoeuvre when she squealed, 'No, *right!*'

Harry executed a manic handbrake turn and threw the car into a ferocious spin.

'You might think about the tyres,' she said, clutching the dashboard nervously, still peering out anxiously for road signs. She was in a total panic. The car was juddering up and down so hard that it was impossible to read the map. She threw it down on her lap.

'*You* might think about the route. Here, are you reading that by braille because *I* don't know where we're going.'

'I'm sure this is right,' she said with no certainty in her voice. They seemed to be entering a forest. 'I thought I saw a sign for a gasthaus,' she ventured, trying to keep the note of hysteria out of her voice. 'Maybe it would be better if we found one round here. It's getting a bit late.' He nodded without much interest. It hardly affected him where they decided to spend the night, he thought bitterly, since he would be camped in his flimsy wendy house with a saturated sleeping bag and a pillow as hard as a breeze-block.

' 'We couldn't slow down, could we?' He showed no sign of hearing her. They emerged from the woodland into the mellow light of the setting sun. It cast an orange warmth on the endless stretch of desolate marshland to either side of the rutted track they were travelling.

'An interesting little road,' Harry mused. 'Well, I'm sure there'll be a Holiday Inn down here somewhere.'

All that lay in front of them was a stretch of glassy lake. She expected him to throw another handbrake turn but instead he chose to accelerate.

'Stop it,' she yelled. 'Stop the car.'

But he began to weave the car sharply in crazy S formations across the terrain, shouting wildly, 'Left, right, left, right, left, right . . .'

'*Stop it.*'

He put his foot down even harder and they careered at break-neck speed towards the muddy puddle where the road petered out, bouncing up on to the grassy bank then shooting straight down towards the water. He braked with all his strength just as the front wheels hit the brink of the lake, tyres shrieking and ploughed the jeep into the water. They both shot forward, then whiplashed back. Sally sat still, pale with shock. Then, as one, they turned their separate ways and slammed out of their separate doors and up to their ankles in water.

She swallowed hard then turned to face him across the bonnet, and articulated very carefully what she had to say:

'This is *my* car. This is *my* trip. We're not equal partners in this enterprise. I didn't ask you to come. You're here *entirely* on sufferance. And I'm *fed up with it*, do you hear?'

She felt a lump rising in her throat. She realised to her intense chagrin that she was about to burst into tears.

He stood, rivetted unwillingly to the spot by her steely passion.

'This was *supposed* to be my holiday. This was *supposed* to be a rest and it's all just been like one long . . .' she groped for the phrase, then spat it out, 'assault course.'

He looked at her, genuinely concerned and helpless.

'And that's my fault? You're saying it's my fault?' His face was all outraged innocence.

'Of *course* it is,' she hurled at him, contemptuously. 'No one

68

could read a map driving at that speed and you know it!' Her lip was trembling. She put her hand to her mouth. He thought quickly. He could cope with her when she was angry but he had absolutely no idea what to do now. She was such a hard, decisive character that he was completely at a loss to see her for once so vulnerable. He drew closer to her.

'A really good rally driver could,' he said timidly.

She scowled and shrugged his hand away. She turned her back.

'But look,' he said coaxingly as though talking to a child. He spread his arms. 'This is nice, isn't it? It's not where we want to be but it's still nice, isn't it?'

He cast around wildly for something to say in its favour. 'It looks sort of foreign. Look, there's a foreign supermarket trolley . . . we could go swimming.'

'Well, go on then,' she said tremulously, 'feel free. Make the most of your holiday.'

She felt him move away from her. She heard the splash a second later, and spun round. He was hitting out for the centre of the lake. She started to laugh, unwillingly. His hair was plastered to his head and he looked like a sedate retriever going after a stick. His shirt ballooned out after him as he swam.

'How is it?' she called.

'Fine. Fine,' he spluttered, 'but then I can enjoy myself anywhere. I'm used to making my own amusements. Oops. I think I swallowed something unpleasant . . .'

She watched him flounder. 'For God's sake Harry, you'll get polio or something.'

He began to make a great show of sploshing his arms. 'Butterfly. I'm trying to impress you.'

'I'm impressed,' she called. 'I shall view you in an entirely different light from now on . . .'

He stood up suddenly. He seemed to be patting his pockets. 'Er, Sally,' he said, 'who's got the passports?' His hand located an oblong outline in his dripping shirt. The smile on her face froze.

As night fell, they pulled together some of the felled branches that littered the grass and stacked them up with the planks from a discarded packing case. They set it burning. Harry staked his clothes out on sticks to dry and wrapped himself in a blanket. It had taken considerable effort and a satisfying degree of lateral thinking to get the car back on the bank. Now, they sat between its headlamps, hypnotised by the firelight, toasting their passports on twigs. They had drained the last of the Glenfiddich and they both felt warmed and mellow.

The mist was rolling across the lake, curling and folding in a fluid cloud, hovering on the still surface of the water. A bird let out a mournful cry.

'That's something I've never seen,' he said, 'that mist. You know, I could really get into this foreign travel.'

'Maybe when you finish your course . . .' she said awkwardly. 'Maybe you'll get some sort of job where you can move about.' She hated herself as she said it. She sounded like a careers officer. Besides she had no idea what. History of Architecture, where could it lead? Probably to a depressing job in some council office, allocating depressing council properties to depressed council tenants.

'Yes, that's it,' he brooded. 'Education, it's the only answer.' He watched the sparks flurry up like fireflies. 'That or winning the pools. How's it drying?'

He plucked her passport off the twig. The ink had all run and most of the information was indecipherable, except that she had once been married. A younger Sally stared back from the photo-booth, looking much older. She had a bandeau round her head. White lips and coal black eyes. She was pouting in a determined, provocative way.

'Very Dusty Springfield,' he said. 'Two flies for eyes. You look a bit sultry.' She snatched it away from him, laughing in embarrassment. Then grabbed hold of his for revenge. He peered up spaniel-like from the page, hopeful and expectant. 'You look like a puppy waiting to be picked out of a litter.'

'Well, it worked, didn't it?' he said, resting on his elbow. 'Here I am, sitting on your hearthrug, chewing up your slippers.'

Her skin was warm and golden in the firelight. She was so much more approachable when she was relaxed like this. A little whisky, the last packet of digestives and she was almost completely thawed out.

His hair brushed against her arm. She recollected that they were in the middle of nowhere and that it was very dark. She got briskly to her feet to dispel the intimacy and began to collect their litter together into a carrier bag.

Seeing that she was preparing to leave, he said rather dismally, 'Right. Well, shall we get off then?'

They drove in comparative harmony through the night towards Boppard. They were no more spats about the navigation. As the dawn broke, the jeep poodled up the hillside, a small red dot above the river traffic, climbing steeply against the broad sweep of the forested banks, driving into the sunrise.

Harry pulled into a layby at a high point on the hillside. They got out to stretch their legs. The Rhine spread out before them, shrouded in fine mist, and the sun bled through it like a big red ball. She gazed around her open-mouthed then registered the click of a cassette slotting and spun round to protest. 'Oh, *please*, Harry. Not Waylon Jennings here . . .' But he spread his hands to deny it, and Wagner swelled from the stereo, in its natural habitat.

'I don't really like Waylon Jennings,' she confided after a while.

'I don't really like Wagner,' he said. 'But it sort of goes.'

They stood together, peaceably, looking over the valley. It was so beautiful there was nothing to say. There was something about driving through night to morning, about the ferocity of their arguments, that made them now oddly at ease with one another. When the tape clicked off, they pulled themselves reluctantly away from the stillness, walked to the jeep without speaking and drove on.

Chapter 6

By lunchtime the sun was so hot that they decided to buy a picnic. They took a steep winding road up into the vine terraces, spread out the food on an improvised cloth and ate in tranquil silence. Far below them was a little German hamlet straight out of Heidi and beyond that the Rhine ran like a thick silver ribbon, teeming with busy little barges. The opposite bank was steeply forested and there were several gothic castles cut into the escarpment. Sally felt a languid contentment. He was all right, really. One had to make allowances. Across on the far bank, a snub-nosed train trundled through the foothills like a precisely-made tin toy. Harry pointed excitedly at it. 'I used to have one like that.' It was true – the whole panorama looked like a scenic model exhibition, everything detailed and functioning efficiently.

Above them whirred a cable car system, ferrying trippers up to the very top of the hillside where the forest began. The only shadow on the peaceful afternoon was the F-111s shooting periodically across the sky.

'It'll be like that back home soon,' Harry said. Sally looked at him, surprised. He nodded as though she might not be too well up on the nuclear debate and would find this hard to swallow.

'Someone was telling me the other day,' she said, 'that the Americans poured enormous quantities of money into Russia at the end of the war until they suddenly cottoned on that they were creating a superpower that could match their own capabilities . . .' She expounded this thesis at some length because it was novel to her and she didn't know if it was true but it sounded glaringly obvious and, if true, extremely ironic. She suddenly became aware mid-flow that Harry had shut down all receivers and was gazing abstractedly into the middle distance. 'Do you think that could be true?' she trailed off, disconcerted by his waves of indifference. 'Am I boring you?' she asked suddenly.

'No, no,' he said in a bored voice. She looked down at the crumbs on the cloth, rather hurt. He sighed, feeling more was demanded of him.

'I'm in no position to judge what's true or what's not true. There's nothing to judge things by. What they tell you's just someone's opinion.'

'Doesn't stop you trying to make sense of the world though, does it?' she asked, niggled.

'I don't have to understand it,' he said. He saw she was offended by his abruptness and tried to explain. 'I'm in no position to change anything, anyway.'

'Nor am I,' she said. It had taken her so long to grope towards her world picture and to be able to express it openly without some man yawning or contradicting or interrupting or saying, 'Why must you always talk from the particular? Why must everything come down to the personal?' when the personal and the particular were the only fragments that women had to piece together. His attitude disturbed her partly because it found an echo in a discarded one of her own. And the 'Nor am I' was not quite right because women *were* beginning to lift their heads and see how the structure was put together. Some women, she amended. And then she amended it again: at least the kind of women that I know.

Harry watched all this going on in her face and misread it for sulkiness. He made an effort to reinstate himself. 'But, I think it probably is true,' he said, 'I mean it sounds true.' He poured her another glass of wine. She cut the crusts off his cheese sandwich.

They took snaps of one another. She set the time delay on her camera and put it on the bonnet then dashed into shot, so that there was a photograph of them both together looking anxiously at the Nikon, saying, 'I don't think it's going to work.'

It was a pleasant enough escape from the tyranny of the jeep's rigid backrests. They both felt the urge to linger and stretch out the little patch of freedom. She pointed up to the cable cars above.

'I think I'll go up there. Get an aerial shot.'

'Oh, very artistic,' he said approvingly.

'Do you want to come?'

'No,' he said. It probably cost money. 'No. I'll tell you what. I'll just stay here and have a look at the stereo, shall I?'

She smiled. He did try. She ambled down the hillside towards the cable car station. There was a queue. Most of the trippers seemed to be from Barnsley. Nice middle-aged ladies in Marks and Spencer cardigans with solid husbands holding their handbags.

As she soared away in her silver cab, the discussions of hotel food receded and all she could hear was the eerie rustle of the wires. It was a strange sensation. The vine stakes looked like so many rows of matchsticks and, as she drifted higher, the varied greens of the different crops became distinct like rumpled patches on a large quilted eiderdown.

The occasional spatter of people pottering in the fields dwindled away into bright self-absorbed dots. She could see the jeep a way ahead up the hillside, looking about the scale of a large gleaming Tonka toy, and Harry staring intently under the bonnet. She wondered irrelevantly *why* he was staring in the bonnet. The loose connections were surely in the radio itself, not in the car's electrics; still, perhaps he was checking the oil while he was about it. She raised the camera to her eye and played with the focus in readiness for the moment.

Harry, on the ground, rubbed his head and stared blankly at the spaghetti of wires that had just tumbled out of the dashboard, unexplained in a multi-coloured jumble. The sweat of panic was glistening on his forehead and trickling into his eyes. His shirt clung to him in damp loyalty. Fool. Fool. He wished he'd never touched the thing. What misguided impulse of smirking bravado had made him offer? He made a decision. Joined the two most likely wires. Then connected any others that looked remotely as though they might have met before. He darted round to the bonnet to see them follow through then back to the dashboard. He tried the radio gingerly as though lighting blue touchpaper. It activated all functions simultaneously. The radio, lights and windscreen wipers all came on at once.

He heard a thin voice calling him blithely from the heavens. Sally was floating regally above, waving. He assumed a false smile, waved with grotesquely reassuring bonhomie. She put the Nikon to her eye and clicked. That was a good one. She rewound quickly for another as he receded in scale.

Harry turned back to the nightmare. He estimated he had a full ten minutes before she reached the serried spikes of the christmas trees piercing the mist. Perhaps she'd get off, at the top, he prayed as he unscrewed the wires again. It was the same sensation he knew of old when he had offered lightly to take the vacuum apart or change the element in the kettle. That certain knowledge that there was one too few grommets and no idea where any of them went. As the wires jumbled down into their previous chaos, he gave them an ill-judged yank, causing the two in the engine to leap and cross. There was a loud report, a long crackle and a swift flare. Flame zipped along the wires, hit the residue of oil in a puddle on the engine and shot up to about three feet of dancing bonfire. It travelled down the plastic tangle and scorched a hole in the dashboard.

Sally became aware, as she tossed up about the depth of focus, her eye pressed to the viewfinder, that the composition had changed slightly and one third of it was now taken up by a billowing column of white smoke rising about ten feet in the air and coming from her jeep. She let the camera down and stared uncomprehendingly at the tableau.

She could see Harry, limbs flailing, his face a pasty dot of panic ripping off his new leather jacket and beginning to thrash at the blaze, muffling the flames and squashing the base of the smoke pall into a folding star. The cable car bore her inexorably upwards to the misty forest until the jeep was concealed from her view by a contour and its position only marked by white puffs in the air.

As she reached the summit, she signalled frantically to the controller to let her continue the circuit. On the drift down, Harry was being squirted by a wayward fire extinguisher and the jeep, still smoking, stood snowbound in a sculpture of foam. For a moment his sombre eyes met hers in mute appeal as she glided overhead.

She clanged out of the cab in the cabin hall and ran out, like the wind, up the steep track to the disaster area. She drew level with him, her eyes wild, gasping for breath as she took in the damage. The tangles of exposed and burnt-out wires, the scorchmarks on the bodywork to either side of the explosion, the cloth upholstery soaking with foam and the dashboard molten and distorted like a Salvador Dali landscape, the dials sitting useless in the strange beauty of their new setting. He waited for her to say something. She looked from the ruins of her jeep to his woebegone, soot-streaked face.

He felt some comment was called for, but nothing seemed quite adequate. 'It's all right now, Sally,' he ventured reassuringly, 'it's all under control.'

'All under *control*?' she shrieked. 'It's completely burnt out!'

She circled it, still unable to believe the evidence of her eyes. 'I only left you alone for ten minutes.'

Harry shifted uneasily from one foot to the other. 'There was some sort of fault in the wiring.'

She examined the charred remains of the wires spewing from the dashboard.

'Sorry,' he mumbled.

She looked at him bitterly. 'You *said* you knew what you were doing. Look at it. Just look at it. Do you know how much time and energy went into that car? How *could* you?'

He shuffled unhappily. 'Look Sally. I could paint it. I'll rub it down. It won't show . . .'

'*Paint it*? Rub it down? What are you *talking* about? It needs *parts*.'

He moved forward, intending to point out how some of the scorching was just superficial, but she pounced on him, white-lipped with fury, and pushed him firmly away from the vehicle. 'Get away from it! Leave it alone! Don't you dare touch it! You're

. . .' She just couldn't give the word sufficient venom for the thought. '*Useless!*'

He became dimly aware that some passers-by, old gents with dogs, were hovering in amused interest. One of them tittered. Harry reddened slightly. It was one thing to be standing there revealed as a total mechanical incompetent, soaking wet, his new leather jacket from Take Six in scorched tatters. It was another to be showered with perfectly justified personal abuse to which there was no answer.

'Look, I said I was sorry . . .' Some children drifting down in the cable car were laughing, shouting something in German and pointing to him. All the couples from Barnsley were craning out of their cabs to take a look at him. One of the kids dropped a yoghurt carton on his head. 'Oh *sod* it. Okay, so I made a mistake. I've said I'll put it right. But I don't care to stand here being gawped at by all and sundry while you squawl at me. I've got *some* pride, you know.' He turned to the spectators and waved his arm irritably. 'Oy, clear off. You never seen a lovers' tiff before?'

'Look at it,' was all she could say.

He turned back to her with intense irritation and began to mimic. 'Look at it. Look at it. You're like a parrot. You're always *criticising*. Why did I do this, why did I do that? It's like being on a school coach outing. You're like a schoolteacher –' He stopped mid-flow with a sudden thought. 'Here, what do you do for a living?'

She answered him through gritted teeth. 'I'm a teacher. You know bloody well I'm a teacher.'

'Well, there you are then,' he crowed triumphantly. 'You think you're still in charge of the D stream. Only, you're not in charge of this particular D stream.' He pointed emphatically at his own chest. 'School's out, miss. I'm off. I'm a free agent.' He turned on his heel and began to walk away. 'I'm going to find a garage. You can stand there and moan some more . . .' He indicated the gawpers. 'Try them. They look sympathetic. There's a phrase book in the car.'

She looked after him, white with rage. Then made a sudden lunge into the hold of the car. 'Too right you're a free agent,' she shouted. She hurled the sleeping bag after him with all her might. 'So am I. Go on, bugger off. Good riddance to you. Here, take this with you. You'll need it.'

He turned with easy grace and swept it up, without compromising his dignity. She lobbed the tent at his retreating back. 'And this.' She followed up with the primus and the metal cutlery. The onlookers chuckled and would have applauded had not something in her manner warned them off.

Harry wandered off down the slope in the direction of the main road, his burdens slung carelessly over his shoulder. But once out of sight, the spring went out of his step and he loped dejectedly along the river, a picture of dogged depression. The traffic was irregularly spaced and fast-flowing. The cars blurred indifferently past his outstretched thumb.

Sally was trying to start the engine. Now that they might have come in useful, the onlookers had dispersed. Typical, she told herself with uncharacteristic venom. Typical of a race that needed to invent the word *schadenfreude*. The starter motor gave a dead mechanical cough. 'Damn, damn, damn!' She tried it once more and the driving mirror wilted and dropped off into her lap as a final insult. She got half-in and half-out of the driving seat and painfully began to freewheel the jeep down the hill towards the main road.

He saw it, out of the corner of his eye, come creaking down the lane like an elderly convalescent. Saw Sally, red with exertion, her face streaked with oil. She was aware of him, standing there some distance away, a forlorn figure, hitching without enthusiasm. She studiously avoided eye contact.

He half-opened his mouth to call some offer of help. Then closed it again. The situation had passed the stage where it might have been salvaged. No, he didn't want to risk another rebuff. Besides, the soft thud of the sleeping bag on the back of his neck had been pretty final and unanswerable. He began to mooch off towards the distant spires of the town.

Sally manoeuvred the vehicle up on to the grass verge, and unpacked the warning triangle and the flashing emergency lamp with grim energy. She threw away the played-out fire-extinguisher then levered out her overnight bag and began to walk. As she turned the curve of the road, she saw a car waiting on the bend and Harry's leg disappearing in the car door. Then his head poked out again, like a tortoise craning out of its shell, and he began mouthing and gesticulating wildly at her to run and join him. She stared resolutely at the ground and carried on at her own pace. Reluctantly, he let the driver go and she watched the tail lights with morose resentment as they sped away.

Harry walked the crowded streets of Rüdesheim without purpose. It was a tourist town, a town of excess – a German Blackpool without *joie de vivre* and without the beach. There were two things to do in Rüdesheim – go shopping and drink. The visitors who weren't jostling the streets doing the one thing were packing the bars doing the other and some were combining both pleasures, reeling along the street swigging from giant bottles, clasping armfuls of parcels. Ponderous oompah bands thumped out grinding Europop tunes from every doorway. Harry peered into the gloom of a bar. It looked very jolly inside. Frauleins in dimity frocks and bodices were staggering under the weight of enormous steins.

He would try to find a garage but first he would have to find a phone. The holidaymakers were bobbing up and down to the music, pretending to be birds. The band all wore lederhosen and sported hats with shaving brushes. And then, what if he managed to track down a mechanic and couldn't find Sally? What if he took a mechanic back to the jeep and the man wanted paying, more to the point? Perhaps one drink wouldn't go amiss before he set his whole mind to the problem. He went in and found himself a seat in the corner. A bottle of wine was immediately plonked down, open, before him. He looked up surprised. 'Oh, thanks very much,' he said, but she was gone. He took the glass and began to pour. The local wine was syrupy and sweet and went straight to his head. The music was speeding up in a crescendo and the middle-aged ladies on the dance floor were flapping manically like chickens and mopping their brows with little screams of laughter. Before he knew where he was, Harry found himself squinting into the rim of an empty bottle. Another magically materialised in front of his eyes. He attempted a pleasantry to the rotund couple opposite and then remembered he was in a foreign country.

His eyes fell on a young man sitting alone at an adjacent table. He felt the need to talk to someone. He raised his voice above the din. 'Too bad you don't speak English, we could have had a conversation.' The young man smiled cordially and lit a cigarette. Harry gazed rather blearily into his glass. 'Schlosses. I've come to look at the schlosses. Particularly the one Ludwig went mad in. I understand he went mad in quite a few.' The young man inhaled heavily and let out a trail of perfect smoke-rings. Harry watched them drift out up in awe.

'Good luck to you, mate,' said the young man. 'I'm from Deptford.'

Harry's eyes lit up. 'You never are?'

The man smirked as though it were a noteworthy achievement. 'I am. Kevin's the name. Corporal Kevin Booth. I'm stationed up the road.'

Harry took in the open-necked maroon shirt, the love beads and the belligerent jutting jaw. Of course, British Army, it was written all over him. Harry proffered his hand. Kevin wrapped it in a firm knucklecruncher of a grip.

'Music to my ears,' said Harry. And he settled down deeper in his chair.

By seven o'clock, Sally had tried four garages. She was tired and dishevelled, the bag strap had engraved red weals on her arm, her legs ached and her eyes were stinging. She was making for the fifth. It was looking more and more like a wild goose chase and she knew she was taking herself further off the beaten track than was wise. Perhaps going straight to Rüdesheim would have been the better bet. Just as she despaired of finding it, she turned a corner and there it was. Hoods over the petrol pumps and an iron grid with a padlock at the door. She stared dismally up at the house beside the petrol station. The shutters were closed and there was no sign of life. She began to beat on the door. 'Hallo,' she called hopelessly. She picked up her bag again and turned wearily back the way she had come. She resolved to walk the remaining mile to Rüdesheim. The Rhein road at last broadened out into an esplanade with large pastel hotels fronted by verandahs. The place had a seaside air. She walked into the first big hotel she came to.

At the reception, she pulled herself together and made an effort to marshal her flagging energies. Claire had given her stacks of addresses. She flicked anxiously through her book. There was one that sounded vaguely local. She checked it on the map as she dialled. Yes, it was within ten miles.

A man's voice answered.

'Hallo,' she said nervously, 'I wanted to speak to Axel Hoffmann.'

'Speaking,' he said. At least he spoke English, she thought.

'We haven't met, but my name's Sally Francis. I'm a friend of Claire Bechstein's . . .' She hesitated, waiting to see if this produced any effect. His voice warmed instantly.

'Ah. Of course. Sally Francis. I remember. Claire's talked such a lot about you.' Her heart lifted. This was much better than she'd expected. He sounded genuinely pleased to get the call. Perhaps he was terribly lonely, she thought. When American friends of friends looked her up in London, she tended to give them short shrift for fear of having to take them to the Planetarium.

'Well, she's told me a lot about you, too,' Sally said warmly. She had a vague feeling his family were friends of Claire's parents.

'All good, I hope,' he said. 'She has not said I let her monstaria die and flooded the bathroom in her flat?'

Sally laughed immoderately out of sheer relief.

'Well, let me explain,' she said. 'The truth is, I'm in Rüdesheim and I'm in a spot of bother. The reason I'm ringing you is because I need the number of a garage that keeps Ford Escort parts.'

'Tell me the damage,' he said.

She began to detail it rather mechanically. She couldn't see why he needed to know. He kept interrupting to ask questions as though he were genuinely interested. Then, as she began to flesh out the story a little, she noticed a plaintive note creeping into her voice. 'And then the dashboard's melted and there's a big hole in it and of course none of the gauges are working and the electrics are all burnt out and . . .' She realised suddenly that she was very near to tears. 'And really, well, the whole trip's been a disaster and the car's a complete write-off . . .' and she felt the self-pitying wobble in her larynx. She felt utter contempt for herself, bleating and whingeing this way to a complete stranger. She cleared her throat briskly. 'Anyway, I'm sorry to bore you with my problems . . .' He protested. She carried on. 'If you just knew of a big garage that carried the spares . . .'

'Enough,' he interrupted imperiously. 'We don't bother any more with this car.' She was rather disconcerted. Well you may not, she thought dispiritedly, but it happens to be my sole form of transport.

'How does this sound?' he asked. 'You give me time to shower and change. Then I collect you from your hotel and bring you to my house. We have a quiet meal and a few bottles of good wine?'

He must be very, very lonely, she thought.

'Er. The problem is . . .' she said, thinking fast.

'You tell me your hotel. I tell my mother one more for dinner. There is no problem,' he said, dismissively.

Now that Sally had his aged mother seated at the table, she had no trouble with the rest of the jigsaw. She saw a glass of red wine glinting in a leaded crystal glass against a pink cloth and a plate of lightly cooked vegetables oozing with butter. The tinkle of polite conversation. The vision was immeasurably comforting after the experiences of the past forty-eight hours.

'I'll collect you in an hour,' he said.

'That,' she said weakly, 'sounds divine.'

Harry, meanwhile, sat mesmerised in the same position in the same seat of the same bar looking unhappily at Kevin who was at the high point of another extremely long and extremely gory anecdote. Kevin had a large, rubber face, gimlet eyes enlarged by

National Health specs, and from the moment he made eye contact with a victim, it was a battle of wills. He was extremely adept at keeping his rabbits hypnotised. He had a way of calculating the breathers between one yarn and the next so that the unwilling listener who tried to slope off could be dragged back at the vital moment like a mouse on a cat's paw. He took one now. Harry seized his opportunity, animated himself from his slumped trance and made to get up from his seat. 'Well, mate. I'd better be getting . . .'

'Oh, that's another one,' said Kevin expansively, as though recalling a story that Harry would kick himself to miss. 'Dick Jones. Welsh fella from Hartlepool. That was the hand-grenade accident. Cor blimey.' Kevin creased up at the thought, 'Only threw the pin and kept the hand-grenade. What a bozo! Can you imagine?' Kevin lobbed an imaginary pin and stared after it, then did a belated doubletake at the imaginary grenade. Then mimed the explosion. 'Just like that,' he said, doing his Tommy Cooper and cackling with laughter. Harry forced a weary smile. 'Mind you,' said Kevin, becoming serious for a moment, 'his snooker days are over, all right. You know them little Polish blood sausages?' He left this hovering delicately in the air. Harry moved restlessly in his seat, a sick look on his face.

'Still, it's a great life, though,' said Kevin, becoming reflective. 'The other day we nipped off with a Centurion tank. Honest! Laugh! I'm not kiddin', that tank was doing fifty. We went right through the village. Then, suddenly, *whoomp*, straight through the barbed wire and then we hit the cottage . . .' He laughed nostalgically. 'It's a great life.'

Harry's elbow slipped off the table. He was paralysed with weariness and boredom and self-disgust.

'You ever thought about it?' Kevin asked. 'You oughta think about it.' He sized Harry up like a recruiting officer.

'Yeah,' Harry yawned. 'I was in three months. I got fed up with polishing everything. What with me boots pinchin', people shoutin' at you all the time.'

'Oh well. Three months. You hardly get a chance to handle the

83

hardware, do you?' said Kevin without interest. Harry opened his mouth to begin another valedictory manoeuvre but Kevin was faster. 'Talking of boots, one of the geezers got his foot trapped under a tank on practice the other day . . .' Harry's eyes were beginning to droop. The words 'beef fritter' impinged on his consciousness. Kevin carried on for some time before he finally had to concede that Harry was actually asleep.

Kevin woke him when time came to pay the bill. 'Nah. I'll do this,' he said with a flourish. 'You're skint.' He brandished a wad of notes ostentatiously. Kevin was a desperately lonely person. This was one way he sometimes kept friends.

'Well, mate, it's been really nice talking to you,' said Kevin as they walked out into the balmy night air. He shook hands gravely with Harry, wondering how to detain him. 'Might see you if you're around tomorrow. Swap a few more stories.'

Harry nodded. Nothing appealed to him less.

'You're freshening up, now you're out in the air, aren't yer?' said Kevin admiringly. Harry shook his head dumbly. 'It's only eight o'clock,' Kevin persisted. 'Well, I don't know about you.' He watched some nubile bodies pass. 'I think I'll go down the Drossel- gasse, see if I can pick up a bit. You coming or what?'

'No, mate,' said Harry, as Kevin tailed behind him, 'I've had it. I've been driving for twenty-four hours. I was in the cop shop before that and out of it the night before that. I've gotta get some sleep.'

Kevin looked at him pityingly as though he was a puny little vessel. 'I've got some dexies,' he offered, riffling through his pocket. Harry shook his head tersely, appalled at the thought. He wondered how long Kevin was going to tag behind him.

'Well, might see you same bar tomorrow,' said Kevin hopefully. Harry was already walking off in the night, hauling his tent and sleeping bag over his shoulder. Kevin watched him weave slightly unsteady diagonals across the pavement until he was swallowed up by the crowd.

Harry had no clear idea where his feet were taking him – he was too busy concentrating on placing the one training shoe precisely behind the other, and keeping focus on his shoelaces as he lurched instinctively away from the lights of the town.

The road he took followed the river and so he found himself eventually back where he'd started at the foot of the vineyard. The scene of their parting was clearly landmarked by the abandoned jeep. In the flashing glare of the warning light, its headlamps looked like enormous reproachful eyes and the radiator grille made a woebegone gash of a mouth. He looked around in the darkness, as though half hoping to find Sally peeping playfully from behind a tree. She wasn't. He supposed she'd had no luck finding a mechanic and had given up till the morning. The jeep looked very inviting. He hesitated. It would be acutely embarrassing to be caught kipping in the car he'd managed to blow up. Through the haze of alcohol and exhaustion, he tried to figure out what the chances were. Pretty slim, he thought. Besides, he couldn't face another night in the open and his sleeping bag was still damp. He threw his bags in the back and clambered in after them. No sooner had he settled in than his head slumped on his duffel bag and he fell into a deep comatose sleep.

Sally waited in the foyer of the hotel. She had spruced up and put on a dress for the benefit of Axel's mother. At the stroke of nine, a silver Lamborghini glided smoothly to a halt outside and a tall, bronzed man got out. She strode out to meet him. 'Axel?' she asked. 'Sally.' He took her arm as though she were an old and very dear friend. He was in his early thirties, extremely good-looking with regular, classical features. He had the kind of piercing blue eyes that sizzle against a tan and he had selected a shirt of the same colour that made them even more shockingly blue. God, what a charmer, she thought. She was instinctively mistrustful of very good-looking men. They were invariably even more selfish and arrogant than the common-or-garden variety. So Axel had a severe handicap before he began. He looked the chiselled hero of a *Woman's Own* romance and she knew from the Lamborghini that they were at odds already.

'This is so kind of you,' she said as he handed her in to its welcoming upholstery.

'It's no problem,' he smiled. 'It's entirely my pleasure.' His English was good, clipped and correct with an American edge.

As they drove off, he said, 'So, where is it? You must direct me.'

'What?' she asked, confused.

'The jeep,' he reminded her gently. 'We were going to tow the jeep.'

She looked at him surprised. He seemed to think this had been clear from their conversation. 'We tow the jeep to my mother's house,' he said. 'There's a workshop there. It's the best we do this now I think.'

'Well, that's . . . marvellous,' she said, astounded that anyone should go to such lengths for a stranger. She let herself sink back into the grey leather, savouring the sheer decadent bliss of surrendering responsibility to someone else. The car purred and she felt like purring with it. She was already prepared to forgive him his looks.

The jeep was a sorry sight, perched half-on, half-off the grass verge where she'd left it. Axel made light work of the operation, attaching the tow rope quickly and efficiently. She got into the driving seat. He gave her a thumbs-up sign and a smile and they began to weave at a sedate pace up the hillside into the darkness. She didn't think to look in the back where Harry, insensible as a felled log, was smiling in his sleep. He was dreaming, as one often does after a long period of continuous driving, that he was still in the jeep and it was miraculously driving itself. Julie Andrews was involved somewhere and so there was no danger. He snuggled more intimately into the warmth of Sally's anorak and pressed his nose into the tool kit as they flew over Africa.

Sally allowed her smarting eyes to defocus as she steered the jeep like a kiddie's bumper car. The road narrowed and the forests closed in on either side until they snaked off on to a smaller private road, then sharply up into extensive grounds. They drove into the garage, which seemed to be part of a stable block. They walked out

86

into the forecourt together. Her eyes moved up the facade of the building.

'God, how wonderful,' she said awkwardly, 'a castle.'

'It's a very small castle,' he laughed apologetically, and led her through its portals. It was actually quite a medium-sized castle as castles went, but inside normality reasserted itself and it was much like any country house at a weekend. The family were charming. There was an assortment of sisters and brothers-in-law and children, all of whom were cordial and anxious to make her feel at home. Inge, his mother, was a lively, vivid woman in her fifties – at once relaxed, welcoming, solicitous and informal. She wore a loose fitting djellaba and looked as though she would have been at home in Gloucestershire in green wellington boots. 'But where's Sally's bag?' she protested. 'But, yes, of course you'll stay the night. I won't hear of you going back to some awful hotel with a train running through your bathroom.' They all spoke the German brand of faultless American-English. Sally felt a pang for the dogged insularity of the British, when every educated foreigner seemed to be effortlessly trilingual.

At length, they drifted from the cream and chintz langour of the drawing room to the austere splendour of the baronial dining room. The arched windows gave a breathtaking view over the lights of the Rhine in the darkness. Gleaming brass bowls of roses dotted the snow-white embroidered cloth. The crystal facets of the glasses darted rainbow prisms in the candlelight and there was the scent of oranges hanging in the air from the subtle incense sticks. As she sipped her third glass of red wine, Sally felt perfectly contented. The candles cast a warm glow on the faces around her as they laughed and talked.

They were enlightened, liberal people. Inge was a staunch feminist, and a socialist, it seemed.

'It's not some fixed -ism, progressing in a straight line,' she was saying. 'It's in the nature of the movement to be a sprawl, to be adaptive. Sure, it's a sprawl, it has to be a sprawl to survive.'

Sally nodded vigorously. There was nothing more exhilarating than arguing a thesis among intelligent people who were all in total

87

agreement. There was a heady self-righteousness about it that went to the head like champagne.

'Quality of life, economic survival, these are the issues. They can't be tackled from the old narrow base. The parties have to face this . . .'

Sally was just about to launch on a favourite theory of wealth redistribution when the chandelier tinkled out a warning note, stirred by the rising heat of the silver candelabra. She had a strange, disorientating sensation, sitting in this *Homes and Gardens* interior discussing socialism. She examined it. What was it she wanted them to do? Give all their money away and then discuss it?

She had been silent for some minutes, staring reflectively at the stem of her glass, when she became aware of Axel watching her. He smiled with enormous sympathy and she thought for a moment that he understood what was going through her head. He seemed a very compassionate man. His heart was in the right place. No, she decided, she would not hold his parents' enormous wealth against them. What were any of them but locked inexorably into accidents of birth and sex and time? And that was true of Harry as well.

Axel was pressing her now, teasing her into telling the story of the trip. He knew the skeleton already and found it amusing. She relaxed into the telling, beginning to embroider it around the edges, but she needn't have bothered because the catalogue of disasters, combined with the free-flowing wine, had them all splitting their sides at her expense.

'*Totally* useless. Completely feckless,' she was saying. 'Then he got arrested for vagrancy. I went down to bail him out and the police said, we'll pay you to take him away . . .'

Axel spluttered and cut across the general hilarity. 'And then he blew up the car . . .'

They all exploded into fresh gusts of laughter. Sally nodded glumly to show it was all true. 'Smoke spiralling up the hillside. Flames everywhere. Everyone hanging out of their cable cars to get a better view . . .'

Inge was wiping her eyes and holding up her hand, weak with laughing, as though she couldn't take any more.

'. . . Walking off like some outraged martyr with his sleeping bag over his back, and that's the last I saw of him.'

When the laughter died down, Inge's face became sterner. 'Ah, but you must never advertise in a paper this way again. He might have been a murderer . . . anything . . .'

'The man was a complete menace,' said Axel.

'Oh no,' Sally objected. She was beginning to feel a little shabby, sharpening her wit on the departed Harry. 'Nothing like that. He was a nightmare but he was a sort of harmless nightmare . . .'

Inge looked at her without patience. 'He took advantage of you. I've no time for this sort of opportunism. It makes me angry to think about it. Aren't you angry?'

Sally thought about it. The funny thing was she didn't feel at all angry any more, only rather tired. Now that the jeep was safely in the garage and there was every chance of getting it on the road tomorrow, her anger had dissipated. Axel had rung a dealer friend who promised to bring over a selection of spares and parts. Now, muzzy with wine, she could hardly raise a flicker of wrath for the unfortunate Harry hitching out there in the dark on some lonely road. When she thought of him, it was with a sort of world-weary tolerance. That was the way he was and, she supposed, there were any number of reasons for it. She could see him in her mind's eye, trudging hopelessly round the container lorries as they fuelled at some service station. Standing in the darkness like some anti-hero from a gritty American road movie, calling up to the long distance drivers, 'Going to Munich, pal? I need a ride . . .' She saw him climb up into the cab of a chromed truck as the driver made space in the passenger seat. 'Going all the way?' said the driver as the truck pulled out, its tail lights flashing as it streamed off into the night. To her surprise she felt a pang of . . . well, something. She tried to analyse it. She was dimly aware that there was a gap where Harry had been.

'The funny thing about travelling,' she said, trying to rationalise it more to herself than to them, 'is when you're thrown together with someone for a long spell, you know, maybe you argue, tempers flare up quickly but the whole cycle seems to speed up. You tend to forgive things . . .' They were all listening politely, unconvinced. 'I mean when one's so tired . . .' she trailed off lamely at their uncomprehending faces.

She couldn't explain it, she just knew that wherever Harry was out there in the black of night, she felt rather sorry for him.

Chapter 7

In the darkness, Harry stirred. He lay curled up amongst his bags, a metal bar of some sort jammed in the small of his back. In his dream a horse whinnied very nearby. He woke up suddenly and it whinnied again. He looked around thinking he was in the Paddington bed-sit with a horse standing somewhere where the wardrobe would normally be. But the blackness was too uncompromising for his room in London. There, light trickled through the nicotine-stained fibreglass curtains with their motif of vinegar bottles and cruet sets. This was the blackness of confinement. He was in the back of the jeep, that much was clear. He groped for the giant press-studs that secured the hood and unpopped them but no light flooded in. He scrambled out and began to grope his way round the room for some sort of clue. He tried to think what had happened the previous night but it eluded him for the moment. Perhaps the car had been impounded by the police and he had been impounded with it, unremarked. In which case Sally would reclaim him, he thought trustingly. Then it occurred to him that the jeep might have been stolen but that was unlikely in its present condition. As he fingered the surfaces speculatively like a blind man, he realised the awful truth. He was in some small, remote workshop on the outskirts of Rüdesheim. The door was unusually stout and there were no windows. The walls were of a soundproof breezeblock construction and it was Saturday night according to his digital display. He pondered whether an economic miracle meant you did less overtime or more. He rather thought less. Which meant he would be here until nine o'clock Monday. He began to thump heftily on the door. He banged and shouted till he was hoarse then listened keenly for any glimmer of response. There was only the mocking hoot of a German owl.

The housekeeper, at work in the downstairs kitchen, had a degree of hearing impairment that baffled the bass tones, so it wasn't until Harry's thumping became desperate that she heard anything at all. She stuffed the fourth volley of endless dinner dishes in the Dish-O-Matic and, as she straightened up, heard the distant muffled cursing. She cocked her ear. There was definitely something out there. She wiped the soapsuds on to her pinny and waddled purposefully out to the courtyard to investigate.

The door was vibrating visibly and whatever was inside was extremely volatile. She paused at the stable door and took hold of a split log from the firewood stacked in the creel. She approached the door cautiously.

Harry redoubled his efforts as he became aware of a shadow obscuring the pencil-thin line of light at the foot of the door.

'Is there someone there?' he called hopefully.

'*Wer ist da?*' she called out in ringing tones. '*Und was machen Sie darin?*'

Harry pressed his lips hoarsely to the door frame and spoke clearly his one perfect phrase of German: '*Ich spreche nicht die Deutsch.*'

With sudden decision, she threw the lever that secured the garage door. '*Ach Ja?*' she shouted, angrily. '*Aber ihr Deutsch klingt doch schon ganz gut,*' and with all her might she swung up the weighty garage door. Harry, perceiving his saviour, sprang forward to greet her. She panicked at the sudden movement and began to thwack wildly at his head with the lump of wood. He let out a loud protesting howl and reeled back into the darkness. Seeing her quarry stunned, the housekeeper seized hold of him and bundled him out towards the house. Harry had a brief hallucinatory flash that he was being led into a castle. He was propelled, half-senseless, through the flower-drying room and into the scullery, past grisly bags of unexplained muslin, dripping red juice into bowls, and up the narrow servants' stairway to a landing where a parcel of over-excited yapping dogs bounded joyfully towards him, the two big ones leaping at his chest, the small ones snapping at his ankles. She hauled him onwards up the main staircase, past a very small suit of armour, towards the landing where loomed two huge, dark, oaken double doors.

Axel swilled his brandy before he put it to his lips. 'Well, Sally,' he said firmly, 'I think you're well rid of this free-booter and his tent. He's gone now, you can forget about him.'

Sally smiled, glad the subject was to be allowed to rest. 'Yes,' she said, idly wondering what the commotion was outside. 'Well, I dare say he'll be halfway to Munich by now . . .'

The doors exploded open. She trailed off in shock as a wild-eyed Harry was borne in, struggling against the grip of the formidable little woman, in a flurry of yelping dogs. The house-keeper let out a torrent of guttural hysteria, alternately berating the luckless Harry and embroidering the circumstances of his capture to her numbed employers. She had the air of a cat presenting a particular sordid mouse, half proud of her trophy and half afraid that the soggy offering would not be welcomed on the mat. Inge only blinked repeatedly as though the tableau was a mere speck of irritation in her eye and would melt away with vigorous irrigation.

Harry's dazed eyes focused on the one thing in the scene that he understood. Sally, standing, hand to heart, crimson with mortifi-cation in the muted half-light. He found his voice: 'She hit me!' His voice came out in a mixture of fury and incredulity. 'I've been locked in that dungeon for an eternity and then when I finally got out, she whacked me with a plank!'

'Are you okay?' asked Sally quietly. He was as white as a sheet, his jacket hanging scorched in tatters, a trickle of blood drying on his forehead.

The housekeeper looked anxiously from face to face. Her feral gleam of triumph was beginning to fade. Sally drew breath and addressed the room in general. 'He's not a burglar,' she said apologetically, 'this is my friend . . . my friend . . . Harry . . .'

Harry nodded curtly at the assembled company as though it were a formal introduction. Inge came into her own now. 'Oh, how silly! Frau Grübe, do let the poor man go.' She repeated herself in German a little more tersely then turned back to Harry. 'Well, how

93

nice to see you. I hope you're not hurt. Perhaps someone will get a piece of plaster.' Frau Grübe sullenly released her grip. To ease the awkwardness, Inge proposed they adjourn to the drawing room for coffee.

'I'm so sorry,' Sally muttered to Axel as they followed the others through, 'I've spoilt your mother's evening.'

'Not at all,' he smiled. 'She loves drama. It's quite amusing, don't you think?'

Sally kept her counsel. It was more amusing when it wasn't your head, she thought.

Harry was seated in a Louis Quinze chair in the place of honour, allowing Sally to minister to him. Snatches of conversations tinkled around his ears. Sally parted his wiry hair and dabbed gently at the abrasion on his scalp. He sipped his wine broodily, trying to peer up at the chandelier, to take the room in.

'Keep still,' she said.

He let his eyes close. He grunted contentedly as he felt the pressure of her cool hands. He savoured the intimacy of having her total concentration on his head. On him. Axel was holding forth on some burning topic of world-shattering importance and the impenetrability of the jargon together with the claret made Harry feel pleasantly somnolent. They had offered him a bed for the night and he was looking forward to it. A big fluffy pillow. Two fluffy pillows and a continental quilt. A big bath, probably with gold taps.

'I've been reading in the papers about these polarisations within the Socialist movements in England,' Axel was saying now. 'But surely the Left must integrate the insights of the Women's Movement in a more intelligent way . . .'

'Exactly.' Harry felt Sally nodding emphatically as she spoke. 'But that involves a good deal more than a change in structure, it means a complete revolution in their way of thinking . . .'

'We must talk some more about this. Perhaps if we meet up in Munich, next week . . .' Harry half-opened his eyes, dimly aware that he was not after all the exclusive focus of her attention. Axel was standing elegantly poised against the cream curve of the

94

marble mantelpiece. In his pale suit, against the pale wall, he made a classic composition of light and shade like a timeless fashion photograph.

'You know, I have some very interesting feminist friends there. You should meet them. You'd get on,' he said.

Harry felt a twinge of dislike.

'Oh, that would be great,' said Sally energetically, sticking the plaster down with rather distracted fingers. 'I'd like to talk to as many people as I can.'

'I'm driving up on Monday.'

''Ere, go gentle,' Harry butted in, scowling. 'That's my brain you've got between your hands.'

After the goodnights were said, they padded conspiratorially up the majestic sweep of the staircase together, Sally and Harry. He was clutching his borrowed pyjamas and a bag he'd collected from the jeep. He looked around him in wonder as they climbed towards the guest rooms.

'How do they dust this place?' he whispered urgently. 'Eh? How do you know these people? I feel like I've just fallen down a rabbit hole.'

'I don't know them. Claire just gave me the address out of her book. In case I wanted to look someone up.'

He nodded knowingly. 'Oh, I see how it is. The network spreads right across Europe . . . they all stick together all right.'

They reached the landing before branching off to their respective rooms.

'And he's smarmy. I'd watch him.'

'But he's charming,' she protested.

'I wouldn't answer any rat-tat-tats in the night, that's all I'm saying,' he muttered darkly.

They came to a halt. She leant towards him confidentially and said, 'Look, Harry. In certain spheres it *is* possible for intelligent conversations to go on between a man and a woman, without denoting sexual interest. Incredible as it may seem.'

He looked unimpressed. 'I'd throw the bolt anyway,' he said.

She shook her head, smiling, and turned off to her room.

'Goodnight,' she said. She went in and pulled the door to. She began to hang up a few things from her overnight bag. It was a charming, elegant room with an enormous plain pine bed. The bathroom was a marbled folly. The Germans went in for bathrooms in a big way. She heard a timid tap at the door.

'Come in,' she said.

Harry poked his head round the door, then followed round with his body. He hovered rather shamefacedly with his toothbrush.

'Could I borrow some toothpaste?' he asked. 'My soapbag got squashed by a lorry.'

'Sure.' She nodded towards the bathroom.

He went in and helped himself. There were marble steps leading up to the sink. It was like some ornate shrine to the god of hygiene. He looked around him, awed, and his face stared back at him from every conceivable angle from the wrap-round mirrors. He came back down the stairs, the toothpaste carefully loaded on his brush like a white worm. She became aware of him, standing by her elbow, still hovering, wanting to speak to her but unsure how to start.

'Is your headache gone?' she asked.

'Oh, yeah. My skull's tough.'

'You're vision's all right though?' The situation was rather too intimate and she wanted to nudge him on.

'Oh fine,' he said. In fact he felt as if his skull had been split in two.

'Look, Sally,' he started reluctantly. 'You're not pissed off with me turning up again like this?'

'Of course not,' she smiled. 'I was worried about you.' She bent down to repack the things in her case. Harry looked faintly gratified at this information. He couldn't judge whether it was heavy irony or genuine concern but he allowed himself the luxury of the second option.

Sunday breakfast was an art form at the Hoffmans'. It lingered on until midday and Harry was becoming restless. He had already been for two solitary constitutionals and knew every nook and cranny of the vegetable garden. It wasn't until two in the afternoon that Axel suggested they start work on the jeep.

Axel sported chic Ferrari pit-stop overalls. Harry tried to give assistance where he could but removing the dashboard was not a three-person job and his sense of the ridiculous prevented him from offering a hand with the rewiring. Anyway, Sally and Axel were engrossed in conversation as they worked. They were both bent over the instrument panel, stripping out the wires with expert hands. Harry poked his head in and tried to look expert too. He couldn't help but appreciate that his situation was deeply un-dignified as they blithely made good the damage he'd caused.

'And this idea that you can just tack the women's issues on to an existing political programme . . . this is a nonsense it seems to me . . .' Axel was saying. He became aware of Harry at his right flank and absently passed him the spanner to hold.

Sally was nodding vigorously. 'Yes. But you can see they refuse to see that the issues are political in themselves. If they accepted that, the implications would be too far-reaching . . .'

Axel passed back the stripped-out wire to Harry. Harry looked dumbly from the spanner to the burnt-out flex. This surely was supreme ignominy, standing like a scrub nurse waiting to hold the scalpel while the surgeon performed.

'But all the hierarchical structures are geared to a wage-labour society . . .' said Axel enthusiastically as he teased out an intransi-gient piece of molten plastic.

Harry's ears pricked up. Here was something he knew about. Wages and labour. He was about to formulate some homespun philosophy of his own when he realised it was a mistake. They would politely wait him out as he furnished some anecdote of Halewood's complicated union arrangements and then resume their conversation with an air of conspiratorial embarrassment. He already felt like a gnat buzzing round a picnic and speech would only heighten the sensation. He put the spanner down wearily, drew closer to Sally.

'Look, I think I'll just thumb into town,' he said.

She looked surprised.

'Gotta meet someone.'

'I didn't know you had friends here,' she said.

'Oh yeah.' He shrugged airily as though they numbered legions, gave a contemptuous glance at Axel. 'Friends of friends, you know . . .'

He didn't move off immediately but hovered tentatively by her. He lowered his voice to a casual but more intimate tone: 'So. Will I see you later on, like?'

She hesitated. Axel pretended to be absorbed in his wiring but she knew he was alert to the interchange. He was interested in fathoming the relationship between the ill-assorted pair. It seemed to Axel that there must be a little more to it than she'd let on, simply because Harry, for all the strikes against him, was inexplicably still here.

'Er. I'm at the Rheinstein Hotel,' she said, in a subdued tone, wondering what Axel would think.

Harry turned, satisfied. He darted a gleam of triumph at Axel like one dog seeing off another.

'Many thanks for the bed.'

'It's okay,' said Axel, without warmth. He waited till Harry had sauntered off through the archway towards the gate.

'Why don't you tell this guy to get lost?' he asked suddenly.

She flushed. 'Oh,' she shrugged in an off-hand fashion. 'He's okay. It's only a little distance now.'

'I think this Harry, he thinks you are a soft touch,' said Axel.

'Yes,' she said. 'I suppose I feel sorry for him.'

He gave her a maddening smile. The arch look of someone bent on psychoanalysing another's motives.

'Yes,' he persisted. 'But you're not a charitable organisation.'

Sally had no defence to this. She busied herself with a minor and unnecessary adjustment to the fuel gauge. He knew the argument as well as she did, so there was no getting round it. In a world where altruism was the province of women, the conscious women, who wanted change, were duty-bound at this point in history to dole their kindness out with a grudging teaspoon. Women's altruism was women's undoing.

But there again, she thought, Axel had shown he was capable of altruism. He had shown her the kind of disinterested generosity that one rarely met in a man. It put him in a very special category.

'Nor are you,' she said, spreading her hand to indicate all that he had done for her – towing the jeep, ringing his dealer friend for spares, helping her with the repairs. 'Sometimes human beings are just good to one another.'

'I think there is perhaps a little more . . .' said Axel, guardedly. She flinched at the familiarity.

'He's gay,' she said in a chilly voice. As though it were obvious and of no importance anyway.

As she cleared up the workshop, she wondered idly if Harry really *was* gay. She tried to reconcile it with his large, dogged, lumpen face and it just didn't quite fit.

Chapter 8

Harry wandered aimlessly around Rüdesheim for the rest of the afternoon. The narrow streets were lined with tall gothic houses in quaintly-painted pastels like a page from a storybook, but the relentless wheeze of conflicting Hammond organs undermined the fairytale. A small wooden train carried the trippers through the crowds from one wine-tasting to the next. The shop windows were crammed with glittering, ornate glassware, doom-laden clocks, highly-painted musical boxes with twee little figures who slapped their thighs or patted hands with one another or fed flocks of wooden chickens, or permutations of all three, sometimes with Santa's sled circling them, pulled by reindeer. Then there were the knife shops – blades glistening back as far as the eye could see, from small bowie knives to vicious, glittering flesh-slashers suitable for psychopaths – all laid out in decorative mandalas, spiralling neatly against black velvet, each knife a slick metallic petal. Harry's eyes rested on the stuffed animals. There was a small pig with a cat's head grafted on and a sad-looking civet forced to spend its afterlife with a pair of limp rabbit's ears. In the back of the shop, the matt-black rifles were lined up looking as though they meant business and there was a mangy stuffed bear keeping guard. Harry was pondering the meaning of this black museum amongst the toytown that was Rüdesheim when he became aware of a white moon shape hovering on the window-glass beside his own reflection. He realised, with a sinking feeling, that it was the spectre of Kevin come to haunt him.

'Watcha, mate,' said Kevin, slapping him on the back. 'Thinking of getting yourself a piece?'

'No,' said Harry. 'I don't like dead things.'

They went to a bar together. And then another. Kevin was more subdued today. He seemed to want to talk about school. It seemed to have been the most important thing that ever happened to him. When he gave the gore a rest, it was clear that he was very young and confused. Only about twenty, thought Harry as they started on their third bottle of the gut-rotting white wine. And after all, what were the army boys but the unemployed in khaki clothes and big boots? Who happened to like bayonets, he added as an afterthought.

'Only time I ever felt part of anything. Only time I felt like one of the gang and they slung me out. It was Mr Gittings. The wood-work master.' Kevin spat contemptuously. 'A woodwork master running the cadet corps. Couldn't even blanco his own webbing.

'I had a false tooth on a plate,' he said. 'Just the one. Came out on parade. D'you know what he did? The bastard stamped on it.' Kevin was positively squeaky with incredulity, as though that sensation of innocence betrayed still shook him to the core. Harry nodded sympathetically, his interest easily engaged now. He too had been the butt of a sadistic woodwork teacher. It all came flooding back to him – that long summer when he had started out on the magazine rack with such high hopes and the autumn term when he had conceded defeat and handed in a teapot stand. The man had practically nailed his hands to the bench.

Kevin regained self-control with his usual braggadoccio. 'So, I stamped on his head didn't I?' But it had a half-hearted ring to it. 'Well, s'reasonable, ain't it?'

Harry nodded warily, afraid they were back on Kevin's favourite topic, but Kevin was in more wistful mood tonight. He seemed more sensitive to Harry's presence.

'Where's the fiancée, then?'

'Oh, out and about,' Harry evaded.

'So you're on the loose?'

Harry nodded. The glass in front of him had just shifted slightly and divided neatly into two glasses that jiggled in a diverting fashion on the table. He made a mental note to fill only the more substantial one on the left.

'You see, Kevin,' he said suddenly, making an enormous effort to control the telltale slurring of the more difficult consonants. 'She's a different sort of person to me. She can't express her feelings well. She can express her intellect okay, that comes out all over the place in great long paragraphs. It's the *feelings* that don't come through.'

'Talks a lot does she?' asked Kevin, bored.

Harry persisted with his very important train of thought. He was beginning to think he'd hit on something.

'I mean, I've got the vocabulary all right. But I haven't got the knack of making it string together. The trick is to make the thoughts come out in one continuous flow like beads on a string and that's what makes it sound plausible.'

Harry reached out to fill the glass, misjudged it by a millimetre and slopped it on the table. He had a feeling he ought to go soon and yet he was reluctant to go while on the brink of revelation.

'It's the breeding, you see, they were bred to bring the whole sentence out in one. And that . . .' He held up his finger. This was the one. 'That's the essential difference.'

'She got bread then, has she?' asked Kevin.

Harry stared doggedly into his glass, his victory already beginning to evaporate. He appeared not to hear the question but he was turning it over. Maybe sentence construction wasn't the only answer now he was asked to confront it. Bread. That was the stumbling block. If he had money, things would be different. They could have met on equal terms. But there again, if he'd had money, they would never have met in the first place.

'If only I could tell her the reason I needed the lift.' For one split second it almost seemed a good idea. If she were sitting across from him now, he might be able to communicate it to her – the need, the longing, the awesome sense of purpose that had inspired his web of half-truths. Then it faded. He shook his head with finality. 'Nah, she'd never understand.'

'Then sod her,' said Kevin cheerfully. 'Who needs a woman who doesn't understand? That's what you want.' He nodded his head to the pocket-size Filipino bar girls with their rosebud faces, their split-thigh sarongs.

'Those ones understand, all right. Well, they understand every-thing that matters . . .' he added. 'For the ten minutes it takes to impart the "information".' He stretched his rubber face into a ribald leer. 'If you get my drift . . .'

Harry scowled. He felt a curious protective withdrawal. A niggling sense of disloyalty. Sally was something private and not to be spread out like a deck of cards.

They stumbled out from the limbo of the darkened bar into the fading half-light of the street. It was alive with the neurotic twittering of sleepless sparrows, made mad by thumping, cease-less oompah bands. The crowds weaved past the open-fronted bars. And inside, the dancers endlessly pretended to be chickens as though consigned to an eternal punishment. Harry was clouded in a great gloom. They mooched along, swigging alternately from the two bottles that Kevin had secreted under his jacket.

'I got one of those for my mum,' said Kevin, pointing to a ponderous dark oak clock, with grotesque rococco flourishes hanging off it in rigid folds.

'Everything reminds me of death, one way or another,' said Harry. The massive, ornate vases reminded him of crematorium urns, the carved clocks reminded him of coffins.

He peered in past the regiments of gonks and mountain trolls to the musical novelties bathed in a soft golden light, looking strangely Victorian and christmassy. He focused on one in particu-lar. The charm of them was, that at nose-level, each drew the onlooker into its own little world. He felt in his jacket for the last few notes. After that there was only fluff in his pockets. Kevin smeared his nose against the window as Harry reeled into the shop and bought one for Sally. It seemed to make up a little for his unaccountable guilt pangs. They stood in the street and sang along with melancholy sweetness to its little tinkly tune:

> 'I love you because
> You understand, dear,
> Everything little thing
> I try to do . . .'

Sally and Axel wandered the winding path towards the rose arbour that overlooked the Rhine. The blooms were full and heavy on the stalks. She buried her nose in one but there was no smell. She recoiled, disappointed, wondering if some fanatical hygienist somewhere had set about withdrawing the scent as being some-how too anarchic and flamboyant. None of the perfect, heart-rending roses, none of them smelt.

Axel was asking her about the conference. She answered vaguely. 'Oh, there'll be a lot of different workshops, people from the Peace Movement, film shows, political forums . . . it pretty well covers the gamut . . . the Third World . . .'

She remembered that she had the programme of events in her bag. She fetched it out and handed him the mimeographed sheet. He cast his eye over the playful graphics in the fading light.

'Mmm,' he said non-committally, 'it looks very stimulating,' and handed it back.

Inge pressed her into staying for an evening meal. She tried to protest but Axel added his voice to his mother's. Sally capitulated with grace. But she was beginning to feel restless. It was a feeling of surfeit, as though she'd eaten too much rich cake, wallowed too long in comfort and abstruse conjectures, remote from everyday life. This was not a real world. She found herself almost looking forward to finding Harry again, to hearing his scornful indictment of the schloss and its kind but complacent inmates. He was the right kind of antidote. Feeling vaguely guilty of harbouring these ungrateful impulses, she went into dinner, determined to be particularly nice.

'She's a great girl,' Harry kept asserting with a lordly air. 'You'll like her.' They shambled down the road in each other's arms, spinning and whirling like two dancing bears, towards the hotel.

The woman at the desk viewed the two sweating drunks with icy disdain as they rocked on their heels trying to keep her face in focus.

'Guests of Miss Francis,' Harry announced like a major-domo, 'Mzzz Francis.'

'It's a single room,' said the woman tartly in German, 'I won't have you up there being sick on the sheets.'

Harry stared blankly at her as though prolonged scrutiny would reveal the translation of her words.

'Clear off! You've no business to be in here. She's not back and you're not going up there.'

German was such an aggressive-sounding language, Harry thought regretfully. The woman was probably saying something perfectly amiable but it always came out in a harsh teutonic way. Italians always sounded as though they were arguing and Germans always sounded as though they were cross.

'Little problem in communication here,' he said out of the corner of his mouth to Kevin.

Kevin raised his voice to be better understood. 'Could we have a word with the manager, *bitte?*'

The woman, who spoke perfect English, but never used it on foreigners as a matter of principle, answered with an elaborate show or ironic courtesy.

'*Naturlich können Sie. Mit dem grossten Vergnügen. Aber ich weiss schon jetzt, was er sagen wird.*' She disappeared off into the back and began to shout, grimly, 'Wolfgang! Wolfgang!'

Kevin swung the register round towards him, read off Sally's name, hared towards the swing doors, gave them an almighty push, ran back, and bundled the startled Harry at a stumbling run up the hotel stairs. They rounded the bend of the balustrade just as she reappeared below them with her husband, grumbling and shuffling in his dressing gown and carpet slippers. The man indicated the swinging doors and presumed them gone.

Kevin used a piece of acetate to force the lock and they fell into the hotel room in a heap. It took only a few moments of their combined native cunning to work out the combination of the Captain's Cabin, then they set to work systematically on its contents.

'You have to mark it off on the list,' said Harry scrupulously. 'Whatever you drink goes down on the list.' He had some hazy idea that a tick would mystically solve the problem of settling up in the morning. Two innocents abroad in a magic land where the currency was ticks and crosses, not Deutschmarks.

'That's the two whiskys, the gins and the jagermeisters . . . and the vodka,' he said, pleased, making neat ticks in the boxes provided.

'The half-bottle of champagne,' Kevin reminded him. Harry peered with satisfaction into the mini-fridge. That left only the cointreau, the kirschwasser and the banana liqueur to be accounted for.

'Woodwork master. Never even polished his buckles. It was him what got me slung out. Mentally unstable! How did he know?' Kevin stuck out his Desperate Dan jaw. 'Too volatile. Well, you gotta be volatile if you're going to kill anyone, haven't you?'

He shot out a karate chop with a balletic twist of his leg, and let out a high-pitched cry. The portrait of a gnarled bürgermeister fell off the picture rail and hit the floor with a smack. Harry slid from a standing position down the wall. He wondered where she'd got to. He had an uneasy feeling she'd decided to stay another night at the castle with the oily baron. The thought acutely depressed him.

Kevin fumbled with the pocket dictaphone machine. Sally's voice began to speak, calm and sane.

'Paragraph 42, section on personal politics, use the quote from Madame de Verne . . .'

'Is this 'er?' asked Kevin.

Harry took the machine from him, looked at it sadly.

'It sounds like her all right,' he said. 'But it's a good deal more controllable.' He flicked the recording switch and began to croon into the machine, 'Sally, Sallee, pride of our alleee, you're more than the whole world to meee.' He looked at Kevin for approval of his Italian operetta style, then rewound and listened critically to the replay. When his voice died there was a click and Sally reasserted herself mid-flow, her voice quiet and crisp in the stillness of the room:

'I soon noticed that the feelings I expressed were turned into jests and that my intelligence was silenced as though it were improper for a woman to have any. Thus I locked up in myself everything I felt. I early acquired the art of dissembling and I stifled my natural sensibility . . .'

Kevin stretched over to grab the machine, bored by the torrent of meaningless verbiage. 'Here, let me have a bash . . .'

But Harry switched it off. 'Better not,' he said, 'might wipe something she wants to keep.' He stowed it away in the bedside cabinet before it could reprove him any more and stretched back on the bed. Deprived of one legitimate amusement, Kevin looked around manically for another. Harry was dimly aware of him scuttling to the head of the bed and fiddling with something. He was like a hyperactive five-year-old, thought Harry, and he had the boredom threshold of a gnat. Harry heard a coin slot into a mechanism.

'What you doing?' he asked, weakly, craning up.

'It says "Massage Boy",' said Kevin, throwing himself enthusiastically back on to the bed just as the mattress rumbled into independent life. With a low, ominous whirr, it began to vibrate in a violent and unpleasant fashion. Harry jiggled up and down, deeply unhappy, feeling his molecules flocculate. The alcohol was slopping in his stomach as though his innards were a half-empty bottle. Kevin bounced up and down with boisterous glee, adding to Harry's vague misapprehension that he was somehow in a fairground. He gasped unhappily for air and the swingboats in his head began to yaw and circle faster than he could watch their motion and then, mercifully, all went black.

'*Acht und zwanzig, bitte.*' Sally asked for her key with a warm smile. It had been a pleasant day and she had a general sense of well-being to radiate. The woman scowled ferociously and slammed the key down like a gauntlet. Sally blinked, puzzled.

Her room, when she reached it, was unlocked and the door a fraction ajar. She pushed it open cautiously then recoiled, thinking perhaps it was the wrong room. She checked the number then allowed the light from the landing to throw details on the scene.

She stood like a statue in the doorway, staring at the bodies of two half-naked men, sprawled like two mating starfishes across the bed. Harry had on his jeans. Kevin lay across him, head buried in his torso, his neat Hom underpants obscenely white under the flashing purple neon. There was something offensively beligerent about Kevin's limbs. Fuzzed with black hair, his lifeless legs were packaged trunks of muscle that ended in spade-like feet. His arms were like blunt instruments. She went over to them with sudden energy and tried to shake them into sensibility but it was like trying to move two heavy rolls of carpet.

'Harry!' she growled through gritted teeth. 'Harry, wake up. *Harry*!' She pulled and tugged at his shoulder trying to force him to a sitting position, but their limbs were stubbornly entwined and he was as limp as a rag doll.

'No. No,' he groaned. 'Don't put the Massage Boy on again . . .' She let him go.

'Put the covers over me,' he whispered trustingly in a husky voice.

She jerked the pillow out from under his head and bundled up the bedclothes. She set herself down with a furious flounce on the hard, upright chair. 'Great. Just bloody great,' she said. She laid her head down on the desk. She didn't close her eyes but stared dully at the tableau before her, still not quite able to take it in.

The homosexuality of her various friends was something she took for granted. Cosy, hospitable ménages in stylish flats with lots of good cooking. A sprinkling of single gay friends on the Scene who conceived grand passions that ended in heartbreak, relieved by furious bouts of cathartic promiscuity. She had always been a sympathetic ear; had never found the single-mindedness of their sexuality a threat.

But now, forced to dwell upon the pictures before her, the two lovers locked in an aggressive wrestle-hold that had no tenderness, their sweat mingling as a pungent male twang in the humid claustrophobia of the seedy hotel room; the neons of the street bars striping their limbs intermittently with dayglo bands of pink and orange, it all seemed irredeemably tawdry. There was a strange, almost animal sense of exclusion, the arrogance of their careless bodies asserting that they were independent of her, of women in general.

And something more . . . she was conscious that underlying her rage was a disconcerting pang of pique, remotely like jealousy. She examined it. It wasn't the jealousy of an adult, more like the sore, bewildered reproach when a school friend uprooted her ink-well and moved desks in favour of a new best friend. It was ridiculous. She quashed it with a little sigh of self-contempt.

At last, she allowed her smarting eyes to flicker closed. And as she did so, an unholy noise began to swell with the rumbling momentum of a landslide. The walls of the room rattled as the train exploded past about twenty feet from the window. The track was banked up so high that it ran parallel with her first-floor verandah, giving the surreal impression that she was resting in some hellish waiting room for a train that didn't stop here any more.

At six-thirty something woke her. She looked around. The morning light was a blue haze, as though granules were suspended thick as porridge in the air. She levered herself up, stiff with sleeping at a right-angle. Harry was curled up like a kitten alone on one side of the bed, his hand loosely clutching the sheet where Kevin's body had been but where there was now just a depression in the mattress.

She went over to the window and opened it again. She had been up and down all night, opening it and closing it, what with the stuffiness and the mosquitoes, the overpowering heat and the goods trains. Harry stirred and groaned.

'I'm afraid your lover's gone,' she said coldly.

'My who?' he said. He sat up, cradling his head as though it belonged to someone else. He tried to recall the previous night but the shutters on the filing system were resolutely down. Kevin. The pathological squaddie. Had he been here? He dismissed the idea as a piece of whimsy. There was no way, however paralytic, that he would have brought Kevin here. His eyes fell on the bottles littering the top of the mini-fridge. The bleak, dull certainty settled like a pall. His brain expanded and contracted in his skull like a jellyfish being poked with a stick.

'Oh no,' he crooned and lowered himself back on to the mattress, nausea vying with rising self-disgust.

She was stalking about the room now, a pillar of bristling rectitude, collecting her things together with the precise minimal movements of suppressed fury, banging the wire coat-hangers so that they jangled crossly, out of concert, in the empty wardrobe. He began to groan to blot out the unwelcome memories which were now flooding through the sluice gates in a rush.

'Here,' she said, tersely. Anything to shut him up. 'I've got some aspirin somewhere.'

She rummaged in her holdall and then in her shoulder bag.

Suddenly one redeeming image came into his head. He had spent a sizable chunk of the previous evening transfigured by a tender, radiating warmth towards her and it seemed a little unjust that she knew nothing of it. Then it came to him. He had proof. He lowered himself off the bed as though from a great height, and made his way carefully to the washstand.

'Look,' he said, picking up the little model. 'It's not much but I bought you a present . . .'

He touched the movement lever. It began to tinkle out its innocuous little tune. He watched the figures come to life. His face had the innocent wonder of the truly hungover, lost in time and space, watching the little wooden man in his yellow hat jerk into action and kiss the little wooden woman with her basket of flowers, and then the little woman curtsey, turn back and slap the little wooden man across his smirking, red-spotted cheeks while the little, badly finished dog at their feet began his silent bark. He held it up to her. She was still rummaging in the bag, her panic mounting, as she tossed its contents out on the bed.

Then she, too, stood frozen in time and space, black creases under her eyes, staring unseeing past the musical novelty to Harry's face.

'Where are the travellers cheques?' was all she said.

Chapter 9

They stayed paralysed in their room until nine thirty, unable to decide how best to tackle the woman at the desk and explain that they couldn't pay the bill.

'She wasn't very warm last night,' Harry ventured, 'and that was before I emptied the fridge.'

The maid came and rattled the door. They both scuttled like frightened rabbits, looking at the door-handle as though it carried plague. They heard the woman's muttered cursing and then the squeaks and rattles as her linen trolley trundled on.

'This is ridiculous,' said Sally. 'We'll just go down and explain what's happened. We'll say . . . you and this squaddie you met . . . broke in and then he went through my wallet while we were asleep . . .' She faltered and tried again. 'No, all right. I brought this soldier back and . . .' She tailed off ineffectually. 'Oh, it's impossible. We'll just have to stay here until we get the cheques back.'

Sally walked out through the reception. Harry took the narrow fireman's ladder that ran from the bathroom ledge to the court-yard. He negotiated the slumbering heap of alsatian, hopped the fence to the street and ran at her heels as she strode towards the jeep. She was bristling like someone's indignant aunt. He tried to explain things, to cast it all in a slightly more favourable light but her terse responses brought the appalling realisation that she had got completely the wrong end of the stick.

'Look,' she said in a voice of firm hostility. 'I'm entirely prepared to recognise your need for sexual gratification. That's not the point at issue. But not in *my* hotel room.'

'It wasn't *like* that,' he insisted hotly, 'he was just someone I met in a bar . . .'

'I don't want to know the details,' she snapped, tossing her bags in the back and storming towards the driving seat.

'I certainly don't remember him taking his trousers off,' he said, half to himself, trying to puzzle out one of her cryptic asides.

'He must have done that after I passed out.' She started the engine. He added lamely, 'So as not to crease them . . .' She let out a mirthless snort as they kangarooed forward and then streaked off.

'I *seriously do not* want to know.'

Harry was crimson with the mortification of someone entirely misjudged on a rather delicate area.

'He was the kind of guy who *cared* about his trousers,' he persisted. 'He probably hung them up even.'

'Was this before he karate-chopped the lamp or after?' she asked shortly. Harry gave up. He rested back listlessly and let his eyes defocus on the barges as they sped past. Why, oh why had he not stuck to the mineralwasser? Why had he taken the horrendous Kevin, with his deeply repulsive personality, under his wing? He could still feel the pathway of last night's Liebfraumilch etched in grooves along each kidney, all connected in some mystical way with the sensation of having an outsize head. The pulses in his ear throbbed like a heartbeat.

They spent the last tank of petrol on a fruitless trail around the local army base. The sergeant passed them on to the Commanding Officer who politely wasn't able to help, who referred them back to the sergeant from whence they had come. He reluctantly agreed to take their details and again denied all knowledge of Corporal Kevin Booth.

'Give me the description again,' he said, making an elaborate show of laying out the report sheet.

'He's told you *three* times already,' said Sally, goaded to breaking point by the man's laconic stare and unable to bear Harry's halting recitation one more time. 'Crew-cut, bullet-head, rubber features . . .'

'Bullet-head,' said the sergeant, his own bullet-head bobbing as he endeavoured to get the loops nice and orderly in his joined-up writing.

'Oh, what's the point?' she exploded. 'They've all got bullet-heads and they all look like psychopaths.'

She spun out of the office and stalked off towards the gate, followed by an anxious Harry, unnerved and anxious lest the MPs should put them on a charge for insubordination.

Harry and Sally stood impassively beside the jeep as they swirled across the brooding Rhine, borne by the ferry towards the majestic bleakness of the forested far bank.

'I reckon there'll be another camp somewhere up there,' he said, trying to coax her into some sort of contact. 'That's where he'll be all right. Up there somewhere. Don't you reckon?'

'I think this is a complete waste of time,' she said flatly. 'Even if we find him he'll just deny it all, and anyway we won't find him.'

Something that looked like a sinister candlestick hurtled from one side of the sky to the other. The transporter's engines throbbed and bleated, finding an echo in her stomach. Her eyes were burning now from lack of sleep and she felt quite hollowed out and empty. Harry shifted uneasily. He knew he'd made one mistake too many and he could see no way to put it right. He put his hand out tentatively and touched her elbow.

'Look, Sally. I really am sorry. I suppose I'm just not a very good judge of character.'

He rubbed her arm clumsily. She let it rest there. She hadn't the energy to brush it away.

'Neither am I, Harry. Neither am I.'

And they stared at the grim expanse of black and silver water, dimpling and rippling as the bank drew closer.

The jeep climbed a steep, ribbon road out of the sun-dappled gloom of the forest into a panorama of bright open farmland. Harry whistled silently to himself to dispel the sense that he was being ignored. Sally hadn't spoken for twenty minutes except to curse periodically in a self-absorbed white fury. He knew better than to offer a sympathetic word in case the little jagged teeth went for his jugular.

'Fool! Fool! Fool!' she spat. 'Of all the *stupid* things I've done in my life, this beats everything!'

He sighed heavily. One could only take so much of this. The air between them was crackling with hostility.

'Sally. This is no good. I'm just getting on your nerves. Do you want me to push off, is that it? If so, just tell me . . .' Anything but these volleys of poison darts.

She knew that the soft, occasional phutting she could hear was the sediment sucking itself up the fuel line.

'Oh, just great,' she said bitterly. 'You wait till I'm destitute, flat broke, in the middle of nowhere with the fuel gauge on zero and *then* you offer to do the decent thing!'

The engine gave a few experimental reports and the jeep bucked as if to prove her point.

'Hey, look,' he said. 'Be fair. Don't make me out to be worse than I am. I feel bad enough as it is . . .'

'You seem happy enough,' she fumed. 'Just a moment ago you appeared to be whistling.'

'I feel lousy,' he said. 'How can I prove it to you? Got any razor blades?'

'No, but your noose is still in the back,' she said vigorously. 'Fetch it out and I'll tie you a competent knot.'

He began to whistle silently again but just stopped himself in time.

As they bumped and jolted around the bend, the jeep wheezing in protest, the miraculous happened. A hotel. The jeep drew its last breath some thirty yards short. They freewheeled it on to the kerbside.

'Telephone,' she said, pointing, and strode off.

'What are you going to do?' he called.

'Ring American Express about the travellers cheques.'

'You'll need some change,' he shouted, hurrying after her with

114

his last handful of deutschmarks. It was the first time he'd been in a position of financial superiority and he was anxious to show willing.

'How are we going to eat,' she was muttering. 'Where are we going to sleep?'

They studied the ground intently as they stalked towards the hotel.

'Well,' he said carefully. 'Now, I know this isn't going to be a very popular option.'

'I'd rather stand up all night in a pigsty.'

He was faintly hurt at the speed of her response. Anyway, they were most unlikely to find a pigsty in Germany. There *were* no pigs. Not live ones. Dead ones were very much in evidence on plates. They came in pink slabs like the soles of size eleven shoes but, as for the live animals, Harry came to the conclusion they were kept underground. In enormous quantity. He pursued the unpopular option.

'It's quite a substantial little tent if you can just get it anchored right . . .' he said.

She slammed into the yellow kiosk.

He sat down on a milestone outside the hotel and thought about it. He couldn't say he relished the idea much either. It was one thing to choose intimacy, it was another to be doomed into it by force of circumstance and with a distinctly hostile partner. If they happened to *find* a pig sty, he might stand up all night himself. But then, he reflected, if they both kept their clothes on, well it wasn't really much different from being in the car together – except that they would be horizontal.

That was the nub of it. All the embarrassment, all the innuendo of sleeping with someone was in the horizontality of the act. That and the fact they'd have to share an extremely narrow sleeping bag. He eyed Sally up and down as she poured her problems down the phone, long distance. She'd just about fit in if they both held their breath. But, as to what they'd talk about, his imagination failed him.

She began to dial another number, leaned out while it was

connecting and called to him, 'I'm ringing the police to report the cheque numbers. Do you want to report yours?'

Harry looked blank, then rallied. 'No point,' he said, 'mine was just large denomination notes.' She swung back in for another long stint. When she came out, he put his jacket on the grass beside him for her to sit on. She ignored it.

She was still buzzing with adrenalin. He could feel her tension. She was like a wire. He didn't know what he dared say to try and dissipate it.

'What's happening, then?' he asked.

'It takes between twenty-four hours and three days to replace them. So they say.'

He thought about the dates. 'Cutting it a bit fine, isn't it?'

She tried to muster her full fury but it was ebbing.

'I don't know what you're worried about,' she said acidly, 'I actually have to get somewhere by a specific date. And if there's anything in catastrophe theory, we're in for a few more traumas yet. God knows what we're going to do in the meantime.'

It dawned on her, even as she flounced down dismally on the grass beside him, that she was actually saying 'we' now, as if they were two equal victims at the mercy of some malign force that bound them inexorably together. Whereas in fact the disruptive quotient was crouched beside her, contentedly poking a frog with a twig and watching it hop. True seige mentality, she thought gloomily. How long would I have lasted in Patty Hearst's cupboard?

The frog let out a belch and sprang from its nest of grass to a handy stone. Harry looked up, pleased.

'Look at his little face,' he said. 'He looks like my postman.'

Against her better judgment, she bent and looked at the frog. He had a blank, bright startled expression and legs like coach springs. The sun was beating down a dry steady heat. There was the fragrance of new-mown hay in the air. An occasional breath stirred rippling waves through the fields of blond barley. Under any other circumstances it would be idyllic, she thought wearily. The frog flipped into a double back somersault.

'Can your postman do that?' she asked idly.

'Not with his mailbag on,' he said.

He tried to set his mind at the insoluble problem. 'Perhaps we could find an embassy . . .'

'There's no more reason for a British embassy here than there would be for a German embassy in . . . Chipping Sodbury,' she said. She chewed on a piece of grass. After a moment she said very deliberately, 'I don't think the full enormity of the situation's hit you yet. We haven't even got enough for a pint of beer.'

'No,' he nodded cautiously. 'No, that's hit me all right,' and he looked so deeply troubled and serious as his eyes met hers that, in that instant, she gave up, shook her head and began to laugh. She had a surreal sense of futility. It was all so wildly adrift from her meticulous London plans that there seemed no point comparing that far-off hopeful package with present reality. All that was practical now was to let go the sense of urgent purpose and enter into the lunacy of the situation with fatalistic calm. He watched the emotions struggling in her face, not sure how to consolidate that laugh into some more certain truce, unsure how to make amends.

'I'm so tired,' she said.

He tugged at her sleeve in a friendly fashion since there was nothing to be said, pointed out his shoulder for a pillow. She put her back against the milestone, allowed the blistering heat to close her eyes, let the distant hum of the tractor vie with the tumbling bumble of the pollen-sated bees. And, very soon, her head slumped down on his shoulder with a soft thud.

By two o'clock, the hunger was gnawing at their innards enough to move them to crime. They reconnoitred the hotel and discovered a ready-pasted toothbrush machine in the men's lavatory. She stood guard against the door while he ran his penknife up and down the casting. He began to lever it towards him so that there was a finger space in the workings.

'It's just a matter of reaching the trigger mechanism,' he said through puffs of exertion.

She looked round, anxiously. 'Here, let me,' she said and took the knife out of his hand. She began to jiggle it expertly to unhook the little spring that held the retaining screw for the toothbrushes and connected to the cash box. She tutted. 'You'd think they'd develop something more sophisticated . . .' she said.

'There.' The toothbrushes catapulted out in a continuous roll and coins showered and spattered as though it was a fruit machine held on three lemons. She smiled delightedly. They both began to grovel on the floor of the urinal. He stashed the toothbrushes in his jacket while she swept up the hoard of money.

He noted her practised manner with growing concern. 'You seem very experienced,' he said, with a note of reproof in his voice.

'Cigarette machine at university,' she said in an undertone as they sidled down the corridor. They passed through the bar, looking to neither right nor left, and out the door. Harry was genuinely shocked.

'It's one thing in a dire emergency,' he spluttered as they reached the jeep. She dumped the tent and the sleeping bag in his arms and hauled out their hand-baggage. They trudged up the road for twenty minutes or so until they came to a small hamlet. They unearthed a small provisions shop and bought some bread, fruit and biscuits, a bottle of wine and some cheap, unidentifiable liqueur. They sniffed it experimentally and reeled at the vapour. Harry put the cap back on quickly as though some evil genie might escape from it.

They ambled through the heart of the forest, clutching their bundles and groceries. It was cool and the needles made a soft carpet underfoot. The sun-dapples flitted around them, dancing on the foliage of the ground cover, glancing off the treetrunks, as though they were in some muted ballroom under a faceted globe.

They came out into a clearing on the brow of the hillside. A sleepy valley was spread out below them, dotted with farmsteads and toy cows grazing. They ate the picnic, lazily; drank the wine, relaxed into a pleasant, somnolent camaraderie. The sky was so blue, it was the cerulean from a paintbox. The puffs of cloud tried to form half-hearted animals. As the afternoon wore on, she found herself telling him about her marriage. His name was Russell.

Harry disliked him straight off. He had held a lectureship at Cambridge. Harry provided him with a black beard and beetling brows. And he edited a communist paper in his spare time. Harry added Gestetner smears. Sally thought about it, sadly, which she hadn't for some time. Her own final year had suffered from the fact that she'd been endlessly available to him, typing, collating, checking his copy; settling into place as the political wife, a faint shadow of Russell; accepting slights from his friends as though they were her due. Earth-shattering rows, passionate reconciliations, they'd all taken their emotional toll. Her dim apprehension of the women's movement as something to do with make-up that diverted attention from the crucial fight.

He scrutinised her face as she talked. The pale straight nose, the cool, sensible grey eyes, her hair hanging in strings like mouse-tails.

It was on the tip of his tongue to ask the one question. He wanted to say in an effortlessly casual voice, So, Sally, have you given up men altogether? But he thought better of it.

She was thinking of how Russell had expanded to fill so much space that she'd dwindled away to make room and how it had only seemed fitting and right. He was happy for her to throw away the Revlon but he prodded her to keep up the joyless diets that kept her looking like an emaciated, stick-legged fawn. A naked-faced gazelle was politically okay but not a fat one. She laughed at the thought. 'And there again, I didn't know there was a whole queue of anorexic fawns queueing up in the editorial office, wanting to discuss sexual politics. Urgently.' She brought herself to a halt. It was really very boring to hear about other people's lives. Harry didn't want to know this stuff. He was studying her with a curious, even stare. Anyway, it was all dead wood. She laughed in an embarrassed way. 'Well, that was my marriage, how was yours?' It was only a flip throwaway that tripped off the tongue but she regretted it straight away. He screwed his face up and looked into the middle distance. 'Oh, I don't know,' he mumbled, 'I suppose I was at Halewood.'

There was silence for a moment. He knew the convention was

that he should offer some confidence of his own life, in return but under the circumstances this was rather tricky. He shared out the last dregs of the wine between the top of his vacuum flask and her billycan cup. He didn't seem moved to speak. She wondered idly whether the car factory was a fiction too. In fact, she knew nothing about him at all.

'What I don't understand,' she said, approaching it timidly, 'is how someone can work in a car factory and not learn things about the motor engine . . .' She eyed him quizzically.

He made a restless shuffle. Here was one topic he had no interest in discussing and there weren't many others open to him.

'Eight hours a day, five days a week hammering the same rivet,' he said, dismissively. 'It's not really a learning situation.'

She waited for him to go on. He didn't.

'Well, was it well paid?' she prompted.

'It was a job, you know,' said Harry with a visible effort. It was a taboo subject. It was always an unspoken rule. No one ever talked about the work outside the plant. 'It was quite heavy work but . . .' He strained his imagination. 'Lots of laughs. Good social facilities . . .' If you'd got the energy to play squash once you'd broken your back.

'Welfare . . . insurance schemes . . . medical care . . .' There had to be. He thought of the three horrendous accidents he'd seen in his time there. The relentless mind-crushing grind, the total isolation from the other men on the line, the tyranny of the trivial set of actions that constituted the job. It was a matter of giving up pretence of humanity for the length of the shift and accepting the role of a human robot. 'Lots of overtime. A canteen that did good chips.' His invention was flagging. 'Tiled washrooms . . .'

She was nodding dubiously at each attractive feature. But then the men were less than robots because they weren't mended when they faltered. There were endless supplies of men. It had spat out his father and his uncle but he still had two brothers there, developing that grey, vacant look.

'Yeah, it was great,' he finished off, heartily sick of himself. 'After five years, you're deaf in one ear, you're a walking zombie, you hate the sight of cars and you still can't save enough to buy one . . .' He tailed off, uselessly, without rancour. 'You wouldn't understand . . .'

She flushed; fingered the blanket that served as a tablecloth.

'You don't think I understand much, do you?' she said flatly.

He couldn't see any point in their discussing it. It wasn't a personal attack on her. Why did she have to take it personally? He tried to explain it another way: 'I've never cared much about money – but it tends to give you a whole different hold on life, you know?'

'We weren't exactly well off,' she objected, stung. 'We were . . .' She was going to say 'comfortable' and then qualify it but she stopped herself before the awful smug word could slip out. 'I don't know why I'm bloody apologising,' she said crossly to herself.

'Well, who asked you to?' he said.

'I can't help the way I am.'

'I think you're just great.' He said it so low and with such finality that she thought she'd misheard the pleasantry. She looked up and caught a look so strong in meaning that the words were redundant. Whatever he'd said, the look was unmistakable. The words were pale and non-committal in comparison. She looked away again as if she'd been scalded. It was so swiftly over, she wondered if she'd imagined it.

The light was shifting fast now as the sun moved down the sky. One moment it was like the purest golden syrup, suffusing their faces with radiant clarity, intensifying all the colours, lighting up the valley like a colour transparency. The next, it had flattened out the tones of the farms against the fields, muting the range to a narrow spectrum of violets and muddy blues, the sky behind a broad darkening blush of pink.

He reached out lazily and opened the bottle of liqueur. It smelt like paint stripper and tasted like Benylin. He took a shot and passed it to her.

'So . . . you didn't meet up with anyone else, like? After *him*. The wild-eyed black dwarf.'

'Oh well ... yes ...' she said, waving them away with a deprecating sweep, 'but, I don't know ...' She took another swig. It tasted corrosive but it had an exhilarating kick. The glow seemed to radiate out from the stomach and make the whole bloodstream sing. 'I suppose I find most men ... selfish ...' She ran through the men in question, in her mind, making sure that she wasn't being unduly harsh on them. '... Manipulative. Emotionally stunted ...'

Harry's jaw dropped but she was busy justifying herself and didn't notice his outraged innocence.

'I mean, they're not capable of forming relationships in the same way as women,' she said earnestly.

'I can form relationships,' he spluttered indignantly. 'I go round forming them all over the place ...'

She smiled, wryly. 'Hardly what I meant. I mean, you've not had any ... long-term ones?'

He took her drift. Public lavatories didn't count.

'I was with someone for six years, as it happens,' he said with dignity.

'Really?' She looked at him with exaggerated interest. She wondered at what point this episode was supposed to have occurred in his erratic biography. She took another swig of the medicine. Instead of fuddling her brain, it seemed to be making things clearer.

'When was this?' she asked curiously. 'In the sixties?'

He recollected himself unhappily. It was either make a clean breast of it or shore the crumbling edifice up with yet more fanciful bulwarks.

She saw the struggle going on in his face and pressed on more insistently. 'That must have been *very* difficult.'

It didn't seem an entirely suitable moment to confess all when the tent was lying like a threat in its neat carrying valise. He shifted uncomfortably on his haunches. 'Look, Sally,' he said with difficulty, 'I mean when I started this, you know, it just seemed like a good idea. You were just a few lines of type, you weren't a real person ...'

'Yes?'

'Look, what I wanted to say. I don't want you to lump me in with the others. I wanna be honest. I'm basically an honest person . . .'

She choked on the bottle. He looked at her, disconcerted. She drew her hand across her mouth and mopped up the spillage.

'What was he like?' she asked, gently.

He eyed her warily.

'What sort of things did you argue about?'

He abandoned the attempt. He'd let it go on too long. He backed off gloomily, without much conviction. 'Oh, you know, whose turn it was with the bullworker, that sort of thing . . .'

She let out a derisive laugh. Then suddenly lost interest in tormenting him and lay back on the grass.

As night fell, they lit gathered sticks and lit a fire. It was a balmy night and the moths and mosquitoes hovered in the spiralling wood smoke.

They put the tent up with the brisk, no-nonsense air of two orderlies seeing to a patient with bedsores. It was not pleasant but it had to be done. And they made it very technical in order to skip over the inescapable fact that, later, they would be lying inside it like two doomed pupae jammed in the one cocoon.

Then they sat beside it, and Harry dredged out from the murky depths of his bag a dog-eared pack of cards.

At one in the morning she realised with a jolt that the bottle was empty, and they'd knocked it back like two derelicts under the Westway.

'Another hand?' she asked.

'I can't,' he said sadly, 'I can't see the spots on the cards. They're all jiggling about.'

'I suppose we should . . .' she began. She didn't want to say 'go to bed'. It sounded like an invitation.

'Get in the bag . . .?' he supplied. It sounded more bland. As though they were referring to some clinical food-processing to do with pre-fluffed rice.

She stumbled to her feet. He caught her as she toppled, regretted it instantly, was about to drop her like a sack of hot potatoes when the Kenny Rogers started up on the tape. It was such a familiar, heart-tugging intro that it seemed natural to relax into the movement. They began to dance, rocking from foot to foot in a circling shuffle, laughing. It was the first time they'd really touched. He'd imagined she might be sharp and hard and angular, but her body, though frail and sparrow-boned, was soft and responsive. And his was reliable and comforting, as she knew it would be. The smoke spiralled up from the embers of the fire and they danced to the end of the tape.

They stared philosophically at the tent canopy on their separate sides. The sleeping-bag gave no room for movement. They lay back-to-back, trying to keep a statutory half inch between them out of politeness, but the very effort of it staved off sleep. They were still and silent, but it was the wide-eyed silence of two people crackling with tension.

'Got any biscuits?' he asked.

'All gone,' she said starkly. Conversation, whisky, biscuits, all run out and no hope of sleep.

'I can't get comfortable,' he said.

'Is icing comfortable in a cake nozzle?' she asked.

Then after a moment, she heaved herself over and turned to face his back. 'Is that better?' she asked of the nape of his neck. It was distinctly better. He stared even harder at the battery lamp as it burned stolidly like a dutiful chaperone. Her hand rested lightly, almost accidentally on his shoulder, like a little bird perching experimentally before it took flight.

'This is nice,' he said idly. 'Like two spoons in a drawer.' He folded his arms with difficulty to confirm his lack of intentions. 'Quite nice,' he added wistfully. She snuggled closer. It was extraordinary how magnetic his warmth was. She leaned up and stretched over towards the lamp. For a moment, her hair tickled across his bare shoulder and he felt her weight pressed into him as she fidgeted with the switch. It felt, to both of them, entirely right as the light went out to move towards each other.

All good intentions gone to the wind.

'You're not gay at all, are you?' she said after a while.

'That might be putting it a bit strong,' he said lazily. 'After all I *was* in the armed forces . . .'

It became clear, despite the tin badge, that he wasn't. If the earth didn't move, at least a few tent pegs were shaken loose by the morning and there was the sound of bells because some milk cows had strayed into the field and were idly chewing the tent canopy.

Chapter 10

She woke up, startled, to a brilliant orange glow all around, not really sure where she was. It took a moment to realise that she was in the tent. That it was Harry's arms wrapped round her and that the soft pillow was the warmth of his shoulder joint. Her head was tender. She lifted it, experimentally. It didn't hurt but she felt the fragmentation of a benign, hallucinatory, cheerful hangover. She felt very good. She tried to make sense of the great, outpouring rush of warmth she felt towards him. Rationally, she knew it was illusory. Part of some primitive bonding instinct that hadn't decently died when the ammonites were squidging into fossils. It was galling to be reminded so poignantly of a kinship with lower life forms, particularly when the feeling itself was so sweet and strong.

'I suppose we should get up,' he said, drowsily. 'But I could lie like this all day.'

'So could I,' she said.

And what would happen now? Would there be Complications, she wondered? He was stroking her hair, consciously and carefully now, as if she were a cat whose nap had to lie one way. No. She dismissed the thought. Sex was sex; hadn't one half of the species been trying to get that through to the other half now for some time? She repeated it to herself like a lesson learned by rote. Sex was a rather bracing aerobic exercise that men approached with the same hearty openness they brought to a game of squash. Men had no problems that way. It was only a matter of packing off the partner at the end of the game like a bag of laundry. Such was Sally's rather confused view of male-female relationships as she lay in Harry's bag with her nose pressed to his jugular.

Now, having conveniently packaged Harry's feelings in a neat box, she watched the sun shine through his ear, making it rosy and transparent, and as she did so, she turned back in on her emotional jumble. This was a man who had behaved badly to her, whom she affected to despise, yet here she was entangled with his limbs, staring in a docile trance at the gristle of his left ear, as if it were extraordinarily touching.

Later on they hitched a lift in the back of a vineyard lorry and made their way to the Bank of Commerce in the vain hope that the travellers cheques had arrived. 'They won't be here,' Sally said, tapping her foot. 'I think we're being rather optimistic.' But, in the way of fate, now that there seemed to be less urgency to the thing, and they could almost have accepted with equanimity another day free and untied to schedules, the cheques were all there in a neat folder waiting to be signed and collected. American Express had kept its promise, and the clerk was serenely unctuous. They both looked blankly at the wallet, curiously depressed.

'Are you sure they're mine?' asked Sally.

'Sign here and here,' bowed the clerk, with the half-apologetic smile of a funeral director.

They hitched back to the jeep with a spare can of petrol. They were in a rather dampened mood but neither made comment, both slightly dazed that the vision of relaxation had faded. They filled up the jeep with dutiful efficiency, drove to town and settled the hotel bill. Then they sat in the jeep together staring at the map.

'Autobahn?' she asked without enthusiasm.

He nodded gloomily. They both dwelt on the prospect. Miles and miles of bleak grey road.

'What's the date?' he asked. She studied the map, the same thought in her head.

'I reckon there's just time if we don't get lost,' she said.

'Trust me,' he said. She sniffed sardonically, and they pulled off the autobahn route at the first turning and headed out for the alpine road that wound up through the Black Forest and into breathtaking landscape. The Schwarzwald soared like a Transylvanian fantasy, giving way to soul-stirring glimpses of the valley

127

as it cut sharply away and plunged. Strange rugged shards of rock escarpments reared up, then hid behind curtains of dark pines. Harry stood up in the passenger seat and let the wind ruffle through his hair and beat warm on his eyelids. This was well and truly abroad.

'It's fan*tastic*,' he said. 'It's like . . . it's like . . .'

He tried to pinpoint it exactly; saw in his mind's eye a small grotesque pekingese in a black costume running behind a Chinese girl up an enchanted rainbow towards a mountain. Just as he was groping for the source, Sally confidently supplied the answer.

'Caspar David Friedrich,' she said. It was just exactly that. The brooding atmospherics of a Romantic painting – black silhouettes piercing the sky, massive, brooding blocks of cracked and weathered rock, and the road trickling through, an insignificant pale thread in a grand-scale tapestry.

He looked at her, rather put out. 'Yes,' he conceded. 'That's probably what I was thinking of, no doubt. Either that or my Rupert Bear annual . . . Do finish all my sentences for me, won't you?'

She smiled. 'Sorry.'

Dotted along the winding road, clock shops began to appear – pastel chalets, painted in Bavarian style with florid curlicues around the shutters. The wares' spilled out around the door frames in fussy profusion that served to make the shops, by contrast, appear even more demure and self-possessed. The biggest tourist traps were at the crest of the incline, with churning rustic waterwheels and carparks for American coach-trips.

They pulled into one from curiosity. The sugary playfulness of the Hansel and Gretel facade went strangely awry as they passed through the door. Before the tinkling cowbells even settled, they both sensed a chilly fast-forward from childhood to mausoleum and no mellow stage in between. An unnerving concert was going on. The whirring and clocking of a thousand mechanisms, out of sync, chronicling the time as it ran away.

Dark, oppressive grandfather clocks stood in long solemn rows like self-absorbed old gentlemen in a grim receiving line. Their wood had an unpleasant, bitter-chocolate sheen like polished dark oak sideboards in a house where someone has died. Sally and Harry walked along the aisles at a reverent pace, aware of the squeaking shoes and their sinking spirits.

'Aren't they ghastly?' she said in an awed voice.

The banks of frivolous cuckoo clocks were no relief, a wall of garish primaries, all performing their frenetic functions – cuckoos bursting out of cupboards, lady-dolls and men-dolls swinging out of doors, fräuleins in spotted scarves kangarooing from pendulums; it was all too bewildering to the eye.

Harry was feeling oddly depressed. In a mundane way, the ticking underlined that decisions were hanging in the air, waiting to be made or not made. He got out his guidebook as she walked on. At least they could eat when they got there. Maybe it wasn't too much to expect that they'd spend another day together. He thought about it. Could they just shake hands in Munich and then split like strangers, maybe with the polite pretence of swapping addresses? Would she solemnly take it down afresh? The Eros Hotel, Bayswater, and jot down his telephone number with the grave assurance they would be in touch? The picture had no real conviction, and he dismissed it. They were together and it felt entirely natural.

'Better line something up for München tonight,' he said casually. She didn't respond immediately but played with a musical drunk wound around a lamp-post; watched its cherry nose swivel as if it was the most diverting thing in the world. 'D'you like going to the pictures?'

'There's a good pool,' he said, 'perhaps we could go swimming . . .'

She straightened up, looked at him, reluctantly. 'Well, I don't suppose there'll be much time. I'll be at the conference.'

His eyes rested lazily on her face.

'You're going off, aren't you?' she prompted him. 'You know, the schlosses . . .' She smiled, half-teasingly, as though to lighten the undertow of what she was saying. He knew what she was saying.

129

'Well, I thought we might spend a bit of time together . . . now,' he said.

She looked vague. Considered the 'now'. Appeared to recollect something half-forgotten. 'Well, nothing's changed, has it?' She faltered slightly as she caught his eye. 'I can't see how it changes anything, really . . .'

Harry reddened. She walked on, feigning a studied interest in the plastic gonks and mountain trolls.

'You're really cool, aren't you?' he said.

She stopped. 'What does that mean?' she asked.

'Cool,' he said. 'You know, efficient. In control. Brisk, breezy, British. *Cold*.'

She made a visible effort to confront the thing head-on. 'I'm not cold. I just don't fool myself because I feel a certain physical attraction when I'm paralytic . . .'

'Oh, I see.' He nodded. 'You were paralytic. Still, you did know it was me in the tent?'

'Of course I did.' She turned impatiently away. 'Do we have to have this conversation here?'

As they walked towards the door, he persisted. 'But it could have been anyone, it would have been the same.'

'Of course it wouldn't.' She swung out of the door in a discordant jangle of bells. They strode across and got into the jeep. Harry started up the engine.

'So what are you saying?' he said in a conversational voice. 'You go round sleeping with people you don't feel anything for?'

'Yes,' she said, curtly, to shut him up.

They drove on in silence.

He stared mutely ahead, his face set. She immediately regretted it. It was the kind of insult men usually offered women and, those times when she'd been on the receiving end, it had always chilled her – the implication that her sexuality was a thing separate from her personality. As though woman's sexual organs were modules from a repeating frieze, quite interchangeable one from another and carefully dissociated from the person round them. It sounded just as unlovely coming out of her own mouth. It also wasn't true.

But her feelings were so confused and irrational, what was the point of admitting to them?

'Of course I don't,' she said finally. He continued to watch the road with surly intensity.

'Of course I feel things but, I mean what good is it to analyse them?' There was a note of desperation in her voice. He looked at her blankly. If she didn't know, it was hard to find the right place to start telling her. He took a breath.

'Look, I think you're a great girl, Sally. Woman. Oh God, I mean person. I think you're a great person, Sal.'

'Don't call me Sal,' she said.

'Oh shit, look Sally. I'm probably old-fashioned but I'm a bit romantic, you see. To me, when two people get together . . .' It was so blindingly obvious he had trouble articulating the thought without seeming to spell out the alphabet. 'There's usually something . . . quite nice . . . they could have . . . if they wanted . . . not for long, maybe, but no one turns it down. No one in their right mind, that is . . .'

'Sex, you mean?' she asked contemptuously.

'No!' He turned on her with a look of aggrieved outrage. '*Love*!'

The word hung there in the air, sounding faintly ridiculous, quaintly unsophisticated. She looked at him, disconcerted. He avoided her eye, abashed. 'Okay, so it's just a cheap line.' It seemed to him that things were in a sorry state when the very word needed apologising for.

She swallowed, spoke more gently. 'Look, Harry. Maybe we *are* drawn to each other. But think about it. There's reasons. We're tired. I haven't slept in three nights. We're in a new situation . . . I don't know about you but I don't trust my emotional responses in this state of mind . . .'

'But you do *have* emotional responses?'

'I think we have to be sensible about it . . .'

He nodded sagely, unconvinced.

They fell into silence. She looked out of the window at the pastel blur. He just drove. Having made the decision to be sensible, she tried very hard to feel pleased with herself. For once, she was one step ahead of her emotional rag-bag. But, as the scenery became more urban and mundane, as the fields gave way to industrial complexes and then to tall apartment blocks, she felt unaccountably despondent. The trouble was that the prospect of not being sensible glittered with infinitely more allure than its staid counterpart. And whatever words had passed between them, the electrical impulses were still squiggling about like invisible firecrackers.

She was aware of a steadfast warmth, still emanating from a hard nugget in her chest, and it was centred on the flawed and hapless Harry. Whatever his faults, they no more affected that blind allegiance than the condition of an old teddy's nylon pile affected its claim on the heartstrings. The disruptive impulse persisted unbidden and it was capable of short-circuiting logic. It tugged with a raw immediacy and arced across the space between them.

Harry made a last bid. 'I suppose we have to be sensible now? We couldn't be sensible a bit later on?'

He watched her uncompromising face in profile. She didn't smile.

'No, okay,' he said.

Before they knew it, they were on the outskirts of Munich. 'Well, this looks like it,' he said. 'Looks a bit like Perivale. D'you wanna get out the town map? I'll aim for the railway station. I think that'll be best.'

She spread out the plan but the blocks of colour only danced about in a meaningless jumble. It was all coming up too fast now. Things had a certain time-span to them but everything was accelerating out of kilter with its natural logic. She wanted to ask him to slow down but he was only doing thirty. What would happen when they reached this little square marked Hauptbahn-hof? She ran it swiftly through. A stiff-necked peck on the cheek, perhaps he'd say awkwardly, 'Thank you for bringing me', like a child being packed off from a party with its lucky-dip bag of sweets. No, it didn't seem very convincing. More likely, he would just heave himself out of the jeep with all his bags, thereby lightening the suspension by several stone and leaving a gaping hole in her peace of mind. She would book into a hotel, ring up some addresses in a desultory way, try to cement a few contacts in an attempt to fill the gap he'd left. What was the point? Would a couple more days really compromise her irreparably?

She affected a tone of easy indifference. 'Does your book have any vegetarian restaurants in it?'

He gave a low grunt; tried not to show that he was pleased. He wondered why she had to make such heavy weather of it; why she had to be so grudging. But there again, she wasn't grudging in her actions – he was here in Munich, after all. He matched his offhand tone to hers.

'Have a look,' was all he said. 'I marked a few.'

They were coming on to a four-lane carriageway. One side was steeply banked turf, and suddenly, ahead of them, the Olympic stadium could be seen, stretching up to the sky, an etched silhouette of glass and steel webbing like some giant futuristic aviary. There was a faint snatch of communal singing wafting on the breeze. For a moment she supposed it was English. She looked out, trying to locate it. There were football supporters straggling along the bank in a ragged crocodile. They had on red and white scarves, tri-coloured peaked caps, and were weaving perilously.

'There must be a match on,' she said.

'Yeah. Reckon there must be,' said Harry.

She looped over the back of her seat and began rummaging for the guidebook in the clutter of the hold.

'I can't see it,' he heard her say. 'Did you pack it away again?'

He heard the zip of his bag swish. He darted an anxious look up at the mirror.

'Hey, don't go rooting in there,' he said.

It was too late. The hairs began prickling at the base of his neck. He could see her, reflected, kneeling there on the seat, frozen, holding out the end of his red, white and yellow scarf as though it were a snake.

She stared at it dully as though trying to make sense of it. Then, with a spurt of furious energy, began to pull it out as though

hauling in a rope. She plunged her arm in again and unearthed all
the other vipers in the bag – his bobble hat, the nest of rosettes, the
Liverpool brochures and, underneath that, the twelve uninflated
white, black-spotted footballs, all with their cheeks sucked in,
crammed together, only making room for the bicycle pump.

With the cold fury of a last trust betrayed, she turned violently
and began to hurl the footballs as him with all her strength.

'*Cheap*. You're so *cheap*,' she shouted.

He ducked and tried to ward off the blows. 'Look, it's not what
you think, Sally . . .'

'That's what it was all about, wasn't it,' she shrieked. 'Poncing a
lift to a *football* match! You're even cheaper than I thought.'

'Hold on, Sally . . .'

The balls bounced off his head and ricocheted about the jeep.
He couldn't see the road for her flailing arms and when she ran out
of footballs, she began to hit him.

'Liar, you liar!'

Cars were screeching past them, dangeroulsy near as he drove
blind.

'Here, hang about.'

He swerved and lost control. The vehicle skittered at a diag-
onal, cutting obliquely across the line of traffic, starting up a
cacophony of furious horns and narrowly squeaking its way out of
a ten-car pile-up. Sweating, Harry swung the wheel over and
jarred them into the hard shoulder, slamming on the brakes and
jolting them into a stunned halt. He sat there, shocked, but she
was quite impervious to the danger past, and still in frenzied
motion. She leaned across and threw the door open so that he
almost fell out on to the tarmac. She gave him a hefty shove.

'Out. Get out!'

'All right, all right,' he said, trying to muster his dignity as he
stumbled on to the verge. 'No need to burst a blood vessel.'
He hurriedly began to retrieve his possessions from the back.
Threw the scarf round his neck, began to pack the balls into the
grip.

She threw herself out from her side and loomed over him,

shouting passionately, 'I've been such a fool. You tricked me. You cheated me. You *lied* about everything!'

'Not everything,' he said, with an aggrieved air.

'I've stood by like a brainless halfwit and let you exploit me. And for what? For what?'

'I just wanted to go to the match,' he said unhappily, dwarfed by her towering passion. He swung up his duffel bag, threw the sleeping bag on to his back.

She mimicked him. 'Just wanted to go to the match. Well, why didn't you buy a plane ticket like anybody else?'

'I didn't have any money.' He jammed the bobble hat on his head.

'Well, bloody well go out and earn some. I have to.'

As he struggled into the halter of his rucksack, the unfairness of it all struck him like a hammer blow.   .

'I tried,' he insisted. 'I was out of work and then I got the temp job in the classifieds . . .' He realised his mistake almost at once and tried to bite back the words. She stopped bristling and congealed into a pillar of disbelief, staring at him as though at a cockroach.

The cars whizzed past, perilously close, the elastic effects yawning past like smears, but she heard nothing for the singing in her ears.

'The classifieds,' she repeated with heavy emphasis. She bent towards him, her face gaunt with accusation. 'How many letters did you throw away?'

'I didn't throw them away. I . . .' he trailed off shamefaced. 'I just poked them down the back of the bench, behind the word-processor . . .' It was hardly worth saying. He gave an infuriated heave to marshall all the appendages into some sort of cohesion, in tough concert with his hampered limbs, and began to lurch off.

'I can't *believe* you,' she hurled at his retreating rucksack.

He swung round, goaded into some sort of self-justification by the mortifying knowledge that his actions were quite indefensible.

'You!' he shouted. 'You talk about exploitation. I *know* about exploitation. I've been exploited all my *life*! I've been exploited by the lot of 'em.' He counted them off on his fingers, beginning to be fired by his own sense of injustice. 'Foremen, convenors, sergeant majors, doctors, social workers, *teachers*, the whole bleedin' middle class. You name 'em, they've screwed me.' He shuffled the sum of his assembled parts excitedly. 'Don't talk to me about exploitation. I've been screwed all my life.' He turned to walk away and then bounced back with a tardily-remembered trump card. '*And* women! Don't tell me it only works one way. I'm shelling out fifteen quid a week on a kid that won't talk to me. And his mother's a *woman*!' He began to lollop off, unevenly.

She spat out after him. 'Men have spent generations training women to be parasites. You can't complain when they turn out to be bloody good ones! What's your excuse?'

He was so far away now that he had to bellow to be heard.

'Excuse? I don't need an excuse. I'm a self-trained parasite. Your lot never trained me for anything else.'

She spun round and strode towards the jeep, slammed into it and started the engine.

Chapter 11

Harry didn't turn to watch her pull away.

He plodded on up the hillside, towards the spire of the television tower, following the tag-end of the straggling supporters. As he came over the top of the steep artificial bank, the too-green grass gave way to a vast plain of baking concrete. The steel girders of the stadium reared up in front of him, rising out of the asphalt like giants' legs. They soared up to support a canopy that draped and folded like a translucent cloth, but which was rigid, composed of glass plates bolted into tensile steel. The structure loomed majestic in its weird asymmetry, swooping and dipping like the outline of ribbed bats' wings latticing the sky. He stopped, put down his packs and took it in. It was an impressive sight. And, as he rested, the chant of 'One team in Europe. There's only one team in Europe . . .' seemed to grow louder, and then an army of supporters began to wipe across his field of vision, plodding in an orderly fashion, waving banners, stolidly wrapped up against the heat in their scarves and hats, safe and reliable – the English lads abroad. His heart warmed to them. The bond was immediate. The chant went some way to smoothing out the creases in his crumpled pride. He turned his face up to the sun like a flower-head revolving on a stalk, and drank in the sounds and the warmth and the fact that, against all the odds, he was here. And he was filled with a sense that, whatever wrongs he'd done to get there, it was all forgivable.

He swung his bags over the fence, then hopped over himself and followed in the wake of the singers. As he caught up, he began to take up the simple repetitive tune and give it all the power of his lungs.

Sally drove without heed to her safety. The unfamiliar trams seemed to shoot out in front of her with a warning bell at each and every intersection, regardless of what the lights were doing. She dodged them more by luck than judgment. Her brow was knitted, her soul was black and her heart was set on vague acts of vengeance that she was no longer in a position to effect. She regretted everything. Every look, every warm impulse, every act of indulgence, every piece of charity – with hindsight all looked like the abject self-abasement of a simpering fool. Laurie was quite right – she had 'sucker' tattooed on her forehead in big, invisible letters and those people with the right sensors could see them screaming on her brow in loud fluorescents. Her adrenalin still ebbed and surged, and her chest was hollow with the dull knowledge that she had been nothing more than a useful host to a parasite. More depressing still, though, was the fact that she fooled herself into believing there was some genuine rapport – that was the thing that rankled. She tried to think of something else. The conference – that was something that had faded in the turmoil of the last few days.

She groped for the dictation machine on the floor of the jeep, where it had fallen in the struggle. Its casing was cracked from the knock. She switched it on to test it. Harry's voice swelled, rich and plaintive. 'Sally, Salleeee, pride of our alleee.' She scowled, snapped the switch back smartly and flung the machine down on the seat. Even with Harry gone, he seemed to have a knack of leaving himself behind like sticky fingerprints. She shot across another intersection and narrowly missed being concertinaed by two criss-crossing trams.

Harry stood with his new-found mates at the highest point on the inside perimeter, taking in the near-empty stadium. The line of perspective down the rows of seats gave him a heady blast of vertigo. He looked at the sprinkles of red and white figures filing round the banks of bucket seats. In the blasting heat, it seemed more like an amphitheatre. He sat down and wondered what his next move was. The others all seemed happy with their lot, contemplating tomorrow's victory. Someone had a crate of lager and they spurted open the cans and began to sway and sing. They ran each ritual hymn into the next one, not stopping for a signal but operating on group telepathy. Harry couldn't lock into it because his mind was turning over the problem. He had a night to spend out and ten pfennigs in his pocket. He cast around for the right opportunity. His eyes settled on a bunch of weathered middle-aged men. They were standing beneath the press box, surveying the pitch. One was dabbing his forehead with a large white hankie. Harry strolled over. They nodded companiably to him and he sat down. After a while, he spoke to the one who looked most like his uncle.

'What seats you in?' he asked.

'We're up there,' the man said, broodily. 'I wanted 'em right up close, down there but you couldn't get 'em for love nor money.' He looked sadly down at the flat green rectangle, diminished by its frame of pink-red asphalt. 'It's like a postage stamp. Might just as well be beetles running round in a matchbox.' He puffed through-fully on his dog-end. 'Where are you?'

'I'm down there,' said Harry. 'I've got three. I won 'em on a Capital Radio phone-in.'

'Oh, aye?' said the supporter. 'What were the questions?'

'What was Sibelius's first major work. Who discovered the Rosetta Stone and who designed Princess Margaret's wedding dress.'

The man pushed back his red and white peaked cap, looked at Harry afresh with something approaching awe. 'I reckon you deserved 'em.'

'Only now, as it happens, through unforeseen circumstances I'm short of a few bob. In fact, if you know anyone who's after a spare ticket, I'm prepared to let two go . . .'

Harry continued to stare pensively at the sacred astro turf, but he could sense the man's instant attention. Casually, Harry levered himself up.

'Tell you what,' he said easily. 'D'you want to stroll down there and have a look?'

The man looked to his mate for agreement, trying to conceal his already lively interest. They exchanged a surreptitious nod and detached themselves from the group; began to troop down behind Harry as he ambled to the lower terrace.

'You see,' said Harry, extending his arm rather like an estate agent. 'You see the superior overview? A comprehensive grasp of the field of play, and yet close enough to the team bench to see the smile on Joe Fagan's face . . .'

The supporters stared at the vista with hungry eyes.

'You'll get a better price tomorrow,' the older man said, suspiciously.

'Yeah, I know,' said Harry, 'but I've had a bit of bad luck with me accommodation. I need some readies for bed and breakfast . . .'

He seemed reassured by that. 'I'll give you twenty-five for the two.'

'Make it thirty.'

'Done,' said the man, quickly. The supporters lowered themselves proprietorially in the green bucket seats, as though testing out armchairs in a furniture shop. They were satisfied. They rummaged in their pockets. Then the older one paused, fixed Harry with a bright, birdlike eye. 'Er, could I just see the tickets first?' he asked.

Harry held up his palm. 'Quite right to be cautious.' He moved to fetch them out from his jacket pocket. 'But you'll see they're marked "Courtesy of Capital" in a . . .' They weren't there. He must have stuffed them in his bag. 'Glossy folder, complete with the Capital logo . . .' He was unzipping the pockets of the bag, churning up the scarves and rosettes. He couldn't feel them at the bottom and they weren't down the lining. 'They're here somewhere, all right,' he said, with a nervous smile, which they did not return. 'It's a shiny wallet sort of thing.' With mounting panic, he began to throw things out of the bag in earnest. Deflated footballs followed one another with dull thuds on to the concrete. Over his head, the two punters exchanged warning looks. The older man's hand tightened on the wad of notes. 'Right Bill,' he said grimly, 'hold on to your Instamatic,' and they rose to their feet as one and walked, with dignity, back up to their distant perch near the roof canopy.

Harry, sweating now with the uncomprehending, tingling horror of his predicament, emptied all the remaining grips out on to the hot stone, and began to rummage frantically through. But no matter how many times he turned the contents over, the folder was stubbornly not there, and couldn't be made to appear by willpower.

Sally stood looking at the paper wallet. It was marked 'Courtesy of Capital'. She had found it down the back of the seat. She flicked it open. There were three tickets for the European Cup. She could have purred with satisfaction. She stuffed them into her pocket and swung out of the jeep; picked up her bags and strode towards the hotel. It was very little comfort but it was some. There was a symmetry about it. Poetic justice. She booked into a room, had a long, languorous bath to let all the grime and aggravation drain away. The grime certainly swirled down the plughole but there was still a nagging residue of the other. She poured herself a drink, pulled the phone over and dialled Kay's number.

Harry walked across the Olympic complex in the fading light, his head bent, scrutinising every inch of the littered ground at a spiritless plod. Men were at work, clanging together the scaffolding for the beer tents, unloading barrels. Harry had already retraced his steps three or four times. He knew it was useless but he seemed locked into the circuit in reflexive bewilderment, like a headless chicken; besides, he had nothing better to do. He would not admit the dull certainty that the tickets were with Sally in the jeep. Because if they were, they were lost to him more surely than if they were stuffed under a mountain of litter at the bottom of the Turkish worker's dust cart. He approached the small swarthy man in the dayglo overalls, signalled that he'd like to poke about a bit in his pile of junk.

The man stood watching him, idly pretending to push his

brush, fascinated. Harry looked up. 'Perhaps when I chucked away me ice cream wrapper . . .'

The man, understanding nothing, helpfully joined in the search for he knew not what.

Harry mooched across to the subway entrance. He hovered at the mouth, wondering whether to take a train; and where he would go if he took one, and how to go about it. He felt a train might give him the requisite sense of motion but he was loth to leave the ground, however gloomy in the dusk. At least it felt familiar; in fact he knew every pockmark in the gravel. Nearby, was a coffee stall with white formica tables on stalks and no chairs. Some dark-skinned men hovered in a huddle, leaning on their elbows. He recognised something indefinable in the way they stood, the cut of their clothes that hung shabby on their thin frames; some sported suits a shade too sharp. Hard to tell what it was, but Harry had an unerring eye for his own. He wandered over, his pack giving him a weary stoop. They were passing miniature bottles to one another.

'Anyone got a fag they could lend me?' he asked.

They looked at him without comprehension. He saw they were Greeks or Turks or Arabs. He motioned puffing, pointed to a cigarette. 'Ah.' They nodded, smiled, conferred amongst themselves, produced one. They tried to include him in their conversation. It looked very convivial. 'Thanks,' said Harry, lighting up.

'*Fransiczca*? *Almanca*? *Inglizce*?' they hazarded.

Harry brightened up, stabbed the air. '*Ja. Ja. Inglizce*. That's the one.' He was moved by their friendly air to let them in on the pathos of his plight. 'I'm looking for a folder.' He drew a rectangle in the air. They followed its outline carefully with they eyes. 'A folder with tickets . . .' They stared blankly, then babbled together. One of them jerked his comrade's arm to hand Harry the bottle. It passed across the table with due ceremony. Harry struggled out of his rucksack. They smiled all round as he swigged as though they'd persuaded some stray cat to take a saucer of milk.

'*Serefe*!' they said.

'*Serefe*!' said Harry. 'Harry,' he told them, stabbing his chest.

He spelt it out like John Wayne talking to red injuns. 'Me from Liver-pool. Where you from?'

'Ah, Liverpool.' They all nodded sagely, pleased, and prompted him to take another swig. They pointed across the highway to the factory complex beside the silver bowl, enclosed with a high concrete fence. 'Bay-em-Doubleway,' they said. Harry read the giant logo, then spluttered.

'Ah. You BMW. You car-workers. *Me* car-worker. You BMW; me Fords.'

The Turks all smiled, sunnily and nodded. 'Fords,' they told each other. Another barrier went down; more bottles magically appeared from pockets and Harry knew he was with friends. He pulled off his bobble hat.

'Thanks,' he said. 'Very civil of you. Perhaps I won't blow me brains out just yet . . .' and he let the hot, sweet liqueur burn down his throat.

They took him back with them to the Turkish café. It was in the back streets, through the red-light district, opposite the main station. The exterior was shabby, with hand-lettered signs and primitive paintings of brightly-coloured Turkish maidens. But inside the atmosphere was rich and smoky and evocative. Nut-brown men, some with whole mouthfuls of gold teeth, sat crammed together, drinking, arguing heatedly.

An old man sang a song with ponderous, cracked melancholy. It fluttered with the catches in his throat and wrenched the heartstrings with its sweet, tortured longing. Harry was quite at home. He, too, could feel this yearning to return to Turkey, although he'd never been there and would undoubtedly never go. He palled up with an English-speaking man about his own age, Achmed, a tall, serious student-type with curly hair and a mediterranean moustache. Achmed translated all the jokes that were fit to travel and as one innocent aniseed drink was followed with one another, the thin partition walls shook with their raucous laughter. By midnight they were all sat round a table, each man staring intently at his football, clutching a fistful of biros under Harry's careful instruction.

'You see, it mustn't smudge,' he told them, insistently. Achmed translated. 'They have to be in different pens. And all the signatures have to be like this . . . at regular intervals . . .'

He held up the master ball, with its complement of the team-mates' signatures. Achmed translated word for word, wagging his finger at them to underline the seriousness of the undertaking. The Turkish workers set to, each revolving his football, pain-stakingly reproducing the loops and squiggles with elaborate concentration.

Sally sat in her room, reading through the pages she'd written. She'd rung a few people; made some initial contacts with women whose names she'd been given. She hadn't got through to Kay, whose phone seemed to be constantly engaged or out of order. She'd spoken to Axel and agreed to meet him the following day. Now she sat curled in a chair, wrapped in her dressing gown, listening to the silence. There were noises filtering in from the street; the hum of traffic, car doors slamming, heels clacking. Within the building, she could hear the whirring of the lift, the occasional low murmur of voices, and inside the room she was aware of the low humming of the fridge, the creaking of the wood against her back. She was perfectly relaxed. She needed to be alone like this. She felt a sense of her reality reasserting itself. After the vivid, empathic shocks of living close with someone else, she felt the need to muster her depleted stores of energy; to feel that she was a substantive form, displacing air in a space. She wondered idly if men ever felt that way. Probably not. Men were usually brought up very sure of their right to occupy space in the universe. She let her neck muscles go, felt all the tension seeping out of her; felt a creeping slough of content smudging round her, when a small, piping, reedy voice insinuated itself with a wan echo through the empty streets and into her brain.

'One team in Europe, there's only one team in Europe . . .'

She found herself moving reluctantly to the window and staring out. It was a lost, straggling supporter, detached from his party, wound around a lamp post, waving a can.

It was not Harry. She despised herself for thinking it might be, or for caring enough to move across the room. She flounced down on the bed and tried to recapture her previous somnolent state of grace. But the mood had fled now, like a transient, subtle shift in the light, and she just felt listless.

The Turks offered Harry their floor. He found himself, squashed up in his sleeping bag, between two sets of tiered bunks, with a camp bed at his head. It was a small upstairs room and, since there were five of them in there already, he was touched that they should offer him the space. There was a small formica table with two glass Bambis and a bunch of plastic flowers on it, as though someone had tried to give a touch of domesticity. Mostly, though, the room was dominated by the enormous television set that was jammed up against Harry's feet, blaring out *High Noon*.

Harry was propped up on his elbow in the darkness, so wrapt in the picture that he sometimes forgot to puff on his cigarette. Everyone watched with the same immersed gravity as though they didn't know the story almost as well as their own. Gary Cooper stared out into the darkness of the room, his face set, a noble mask of impassive granite – a man torn by an impossible dilemma. Then Grace Kelly, indomitable and rigid, asserting the immutability of her beliefs. And the haunting theme song tugging a plangent reverberation in the chest cavity. As the final music rose, the street was revealed with the townspeople flocking gladly out from their hiding places; Gary Cooper tossed down his badge; Grace Kelly swirled into his arms, her hair a thick, staid crown of braids, and he crushed her into him. 'Do not forsake me, oh my darlin', although you're grievin', I can't be leavin' until I shoot Frank Miller dead . . . wait along, wait alohong . . .'

'*The End*' rolled up over the image of the two people locked together in a timeless embrace as their buggy drove away. Harry took a long draw on his cigarette. Someone leaned forward and switched off the set. It flickered away and they were plunged into the dim light from a mean reading-lamp. Harry turned to his friend on the bunk. 'Ah, those were the days, eh, Achmed?' he said. 'When the little woman gave up her principles for love . . .'

Achmed smiled, absently. Harry noticed that he was engrossed in something else. 'What you writing?' he asked.

'To my wife, back home,' he said.

Shortly after the light went out and the men climbed into their bunks and went to sleep, crammed together like animals in a crate.

Chapter 12

The day dawned bright and sunny. Axel arrived at nine, unnervingly vibrant, gleaming with good health and full of plans. He wore a cream linen suit that lent his tan a golden glow, and made the white, even teeth of his effortless smile quite dazzling.

'So, I show you round some sights – Marienplatz, the town clock; the Englische Garten; perhaps we go to Schwabing . . .' he said, as they got in the jeep. 'Then, this afternoon, I take you to Barbara's place, and maybe Astrid will be there. These are very stimulating women with quite interesting perspectives.'

They drove round the city, stopping at places of interest. But from what she saw of Munich that morning, there was no sign that anything of any moment had ever happened there; she was too tactful to ask. She wanted to see the famous steps where Hitler made his speeches, but she wasn't sure whether this was gauche, or even rude. He was eager to show the postwar achievements, not the ghosts, but how could one walk around Munich without a few spectres obtruding? With one section of the meat of its history missing, it made a rather bland sandwich.

'But what about the *history*?' she asked.

'Ah, the history,' he said. 'The BMW museum,' and he swung the jeep round and drove out towards the Olympic complex. Her heart sank at the thought of looking at cars. She was sick to death of cars. The BMW museum was a windowless silver bowl, nestling beside the factory gates like an alien spacecraft. Inside, it was as black as velvet. They picked up headphones and plugged into the banks of video recorders that lined the path of their spiral upwards. As they wandered up the corkscrew, past early BMWs plastered to the walls like elegant flies, past bizarre plaster tableaux of twentieth-century history, the flash of a hundred or so film loops strobed the darkness like incendiaries. The leaking commentaries, the jingling music and the electronic hum combined in an eerie, disorientating cacophony. As the floors helter-skeltered into the apex of the building, the film histories became more compelling, the Weimar currency being carried in wheelbarrows, the Jewish shops and businesses in flames, the rise of Nazism, the burning of books and the Final Solution, all in multiple images. They reached the top, and descended the escalator that brought them down into a scale model of Munich, spread out before them like a real city, giving her the sensation of landing gently from the air like a deflating balloon.

They walked out, blinking into the harsh sunlight, trying to accustom their eyes. She felt rather as though she had been force-fed the history now and was suffering from mental indigestion. Some car workers were shambling towards the factory for a change of shift, and across the bridge the fans were filing in long tri-coloured ribbons towards a mass of red and white.

'You'd like to see the complex, before it gets too crowded?'

He led her across towards the Olympic village, laid out like a fantasy colony on a moonscape. 'All this – it was just a dismal stretch of wasteland,' he said, stretching his arm. 'Even the river is artificial.'

She admired the breadth of vision, approved the integration of the buildings into the overall land-mass, the bravura strokes and yet the human scale. They paused at the postcard stall. Fans were crowding on the perimeter of the stadium, singing, waving sashes, staggering from one beer tent to the next in a seething mêlée. There was a crackling static in the air. Mounted policemen trotted through the crowds, marshalling the ranks.

'See,' he said, leafing through a photo-book. 'This is the Hofbrauhaus. You like to see it?' She was gazing distractedly into some middle distance, her mouth half-open.

'Or perhaps you prefer to have a bite to eat?'

He tried to follow the line of her gaze, but all he saw was a mass of supporters weaving in and out of one another, and four louts sprinkling each other with their beer cans. He didn't have the

148

benefit of her selective vision. All she saw was Harry, in his football garb, standing by the gate. There was a handsome Turkish boy beside him. Harry was holding aloft a football, and the Turk stood by, clutching Harry's duffel bag, ready to bring out a replacement.

'One only,' he barked. 'Buy your kids a little bit of history. Signed individually by every one of the team. Completely authentic. You won't get another chance like this. I'll take a tenner for it . . .'

No one was buying; rather they swerved around him just as they skirted the ticket touts.

'See . . . Kenny Dalglish. Only a tenner . . .'

Then he caught her eye. She saw the furtive glaze of a cornered animal, and then a look of such direct appeal that she almost forgot Axel was beside her.

'Sally,' Axel was saying, insistently, in a peevish tone. 'Would you like that?' She recollected herself. Harry took in Axel at her elbow; the protective hand moving to guide her gently off. Then his eyes let her go and he picked up his patter, effortlessly, as though he had never faltered.

'Yes, that would be nice,' she said. She turned on her heel; they walked away from the stadium and drove to the city centre.

The restaurant was a ponderous, oak-panelled affair that made gloomy evening out of day. Men with gnarled faces and wearing lederhosen sat with ladies in demure aproned frocks. Eel-like fish circled through the bubbles of the fish-tank with a defeatist air. It was hard to tell if they were decorative or awaiting a knock on the head in the kitchen. She couldn't get out of her head the look that had passed between them. His mute appeal. She wanted to feel malicious satisfaction. In fact she tried, but it wasn't welling easily.

And then the food arrived.

'Are you sure you wouldn't like some?' he asked, indicating his sausage. She averted her gaze politely from the bloated pink bludgeon, crammed with its blobs of blood-vessel and wrapped in something's bladder. It wallowed in a seeping pool of sauerkraut and she wanted to avoid its eye if at all possible.

'I'm a vegetarian,' she said, curling her lip politely so that it was halfway to a smile.

'Ah, yes. Personally I do not sympathise too much with this . . .' He made an incision in his sausage so that the skin winked and the meat blurted out. '. . . this vegetarianism . . .'

'I don't think it's right that any animal should be born to be a sausage or a hamburger,' she said apologetically. 'I just have trouble seeing animals as slabs of walking meat.' She always avoided the subject when dining with meat-eaters and thought they might give her the same consideration. No such luck. Axel smiled as though they were about to start an enjoyable debate:

'But there is so much *human* suffering in the world . . .'

She smiled. She knew this argument. The intellectual Principle of Parsimony. Only so much compassion to go round so don't waste it where it pays no dividends. She began to expound the counter-thesis in a mechanical fashion. He watched her as she talked. People were never so magnetic, he thought, as when they were totally concentrated, totally centred on doing or saying something they believed. His eyes roamed over her pale skin, her pale strawberry hair. Sometimes that kind of colouring made a woman seem insubstantial and insipid, but Sally had an intensity that overcame her pallid prettiness. He found feminists very challenging. The ones he knew were all, like Sally, tall, thin, angular roses with serious, aesthetic faces who *cared* about things. He liked the boyish quality combined with the sense of an intellect. And most of all, he liked the fact that all the feminists he knew were quite self-sufficient and did not expect to be seen at regular intervals, courted, wooed or married. He heartily approved of a feminism that created strong, beautiful women who made no emotional demands. He had come unstuck with Claire simply because her brittle, assertive exterior hid a mass of seething insecurities like the soft underbelly of a mollusc. Sally, however, was solid, capable and self-assured, reassuringly free of vulnerabilities and self-doubt. She came to an abrupt halt, aware that his attention was only half-engaged. She felt rather cross. If *he* wasn't interested, she wondered for whose benefit she was speaking. Certainly not her own.

She was feeling oddly tetchy and hoped he would let the subject drop. Her mood was not improved by the moronic chanting of 'Liverpool, Liverpool' that occasionally erupted past the window. He came in on her thoughts as though he'd followed her argument. 'But animals aren't human . . . they don't feel things in the same way as . . .' She cut across him impatiently, thinking that if she could spit out the line of thinking in one succinct gobbet, she might be able to get on with her salad. 'That's what they said about the workers in Victorian England. It was comfortable to believe in their dull sensibilities, in order to exploit them.'

'Well true, that's true. But, according to behaviourist theory, animals are not . . .'

'People choose to believe what they like about the feelings of animals so that their consciences won't interfere with their sausages.'

He stared at her. This was not at all the gentle, teasing playful spat he'd envisaged. He'd hoped to provoke a few light parries, some invigorating cut and thrust and a witty resolution. She seemed to be getting quite het-up and rather snappy.

'Come to think of it,' she said, 'that's how generations of men have reconciled their treatment of women. In fact that's how I just ended up three hundred pounds out of pocket carting some creep to a *football* match . . .'

Ah, so that was it. Axel moved in smoothly to reassure her. 'But not all men are this way,' he said. 'There are some men . . . I admit we haven't got very far. There are many layers to peel off, but some men are trying to put that balance right. I don't say I'm perfect in any way . . .'

She looked at his perfect face, the perfect blue-white shirt no doubt just back from being laundered in some sweatshop.

'It's not in men's *interests* to peel them off,' she said, passionately. 'It's too much to their benefit to maintain the status quo.'

He began to feel a trifle nettled with her misaimed vehemence.

He didn't even *like* football. He held his hands up, defensively, in a joky sort of way.

'All right, Sally, but I'm not this Harry character.'

She stopped herself short. Of course he wasn't. It was unfair to take her annoyance out on him. She smiled warmly at him and let the feeling ebb.

'No, I'm sorry.' She had a quite charming smile. It lit up her whole face and gave her features warmth. It moved him now to press on with his advantage.

'And if you let me know you better . . .' He paused pointedly. 'Perhaps I could show you just how different some men can be.'

Sally stiffened, taken off guard.

Impervious to the minute messages her body was giving out, he leaned forward confidently and looked her boldly in the eyes.

'Look, Sally, I want to be frank. I could wait for the candlelit dinner, play these conversation games, but I think you're too intelligent for that. I'm not into manipulation. No tricks. I would like to have an affair with you.'

She coloured and studied her lettuce. He leaned back, sure that he had played the right hand.

'But, then I'm sure you know all this already.'

Why else would he have bothered to talk politics with her at such length? Why would he have gone to the effort of towing her car, had it not been for an instant, animal attraction?

She swallowed hard; thought back, feeling immediately at fault. Perhaps she had been a shade too warm in her dealings with him, but then she was a warm person, and he had made her feel at ease, she told herself. Perhaps she should have seen that no one could conceivably bother to engage her mind unless it was a route to her body. Perhaps it was the most extreme conceit on her part to have imagined anything else. These thoughts struggled across her face, painfully transparent. Axel continued to smile challengingly at her, awaiting the formality of her considered nod. She looked up, slowly, agonizingly embarrassed.

'No, I don't. I didn't. I mean, you see . . . I didn't realise we were having conversation games,' she said earnestly, 'I just thought we were having . . .' She searched around in her mind for the word. 'Conversations.'

His smile only tightened fractionally. He looked at her with a rather pitying air.

'I appreciate your honesty, Axel,' she said with an effort. 'It's very flattering, but . . . er . . . I think I should allow myself some . . . space . . .'

She chose the word for its seventies tang of liberal self-seeking. She found it rather in keeping with the tone of his insulting little bargain. And then, was it really insulting? Perhaps she should admire his frankness. If so, he would have to respect hers also. Perhaps this was just a formality to be got out of the way. They would laugh and . . .

She studied his face. No.

Axel continued to smile but it was both cordial and cold.

'It's your privilege, that's why I lay my cards on the table. There's no more to be said.'

Then to cover the uneasiness, he pushed the meal away from him, dramatically.

'Look, I leave the sausage,' he said, with an attempt at lightness. 'I don't exploit this little pig any more.'

'Oh, I didn't mean to spoil your food. Please finish your meal. Go ahead . . .' She was terribly flustered. He was offended and there seemed nothing to say. She tailed off, ineffectually. 'You might as well, the thing's dead now, anyway.'

They waited in the street at the taxi rank. The prospect of the stimulating Barbara and Astrid had mysteriously evaporated. Axel hailed the first cab.

'I hope we're still friends,' she said, at a loss how to salvage the situation.

He kissed her cheek, perfunctorily. 'Of course.' Then as he leaned into the yellow taxi, he said, 'But, if I may give you some advice, Sally. You give off some very confusing signals. I should watch that if I were you . . .' The cab drove off. Sally was left standing on the kerb, her face white with dawning anger.

She noticed as she stormed along the road that the streets were beginning to empty now. There were only a few fans to be seen and they were all walking fast, leaving behind them, in true English fashion, wakes of litter to mar the pristine pavement. She found herself thinking that it must be near to kick-off time. She walked crossly through the arcade of closed shops in a short cut to the cul-de-sac where the jeep was parked. Her route was lined with the most extravagantly vulgar fur coats she had ever seen. There were armies and armies of animals on coat-hangers as far back as the eye could see. The plaster mannequins sneered smugly in their hideous, over-fussy creations of chevroned mink, overlapping inlays of weasel with lynx collars and cuffs and fox-eye buttons. Not only was it a lavish squandering of life, it was also such a paean to conspicuous consumption that she felt an unaccustomed urge to lob a brick at the window and scatter the smirking dolls like ninepins. It was as though the sight threw a microswitch in her brain. And, actually, although she did not examine it, it was very little to do with animals at all. She emerged from the arcade without having done any damage and nearly wrenched off the door handle getting into the jeep.

Chapter 13

The game had started. Harry ran back and forth in the settling blue haze, pursuing the last of the fans, wild-eyed, as they filed past him through the gate.

'Got a ticket, mate? Anyone got a ticket?' he implored, brandishing some notes, but they hardly heard him in their rush. He turned and pleaded with the security guards but they were politely unresponsive. He tore his hair. The light was fading and the floodlights gave a strange luminous sparkle to the air. When the first great overpowering roar went up, Harry stretched up on his tiptoes, as though the inch might magically let him see. He pirouetted in agony, threw down his duffel bag, and kicked it with all his strength. He loped off, a forlorn figure, kicking up the papers and the cans, pacing round the perimeter, eyeing the fence. The stalwart girders were designed to lean at an angle that made ascent virtually impossible. They were planted cunningly in bushy banks that fell steeply away, so that anyone foolhardy enough to climb risked dropping twelve feet and impaling himself on a thorny thicket. As the roar swelled again, Harry threw his leg over the girder and began to shin up with the manic single-mindedness born of total desperation.

Sally parked the jeep and jumped out. The crowd was roaring. She made her way to the gate, and then on round the perimeter. Maybe he'd managed to get himself a ticket. If not, she had her speech prepared. 'Here, if it's so important to you, you'd better have them.' She rehearsed it again in her mind as she strode on, giving it just the right touch of ungracious asperity, when she spotted a figure, hanging limply from the girder, looking in the gloom like an unhappy fruit-bat. He was sweating profusely from the superhuman effort and had not the strength to swing himself back on to the girder nor the fatalism needed to drop to the ground. She started to say 'If it's so important . . .' but it had no bite when addressed to someone suspended in the air like a monkey on a stick. He saw her, let go his hold, dropped at her feet. He reared up and gripped her arm like a drowning man boarding a life raft.

'Quick, it's started! It's started,' he shouted, and dragged her with him at breakneck speed.

'Harry,' she squealed as they ran, 'I don't *like* football.' But he forced her protesting through the turnstile and suddenly they were in.

They skidded to a halt. Her mouth dropped open. The stadium was spread out before them, a great pulsating mass of colour and noise; an atmosphere so high and electric and exalted that it was difficult not to stagger and reach out for some support. They stood still for a moment, just to get their bearings in the dizzy rush of disorientation. Sally realised then, as the crowd moved as one to its feet, as the noise level peaked so high it flattened out into a wall of humming, that she'd been under a misapprehension. This wasn't football, it was religion.

The whole experience was like some strange, remote dream. The fever pitch of the noise alone carried her with it – the turbulent, uproarious torrent, so overpowering that it seemed to be tangible, visible in the aura of the floodlights. The supporters were just a sea of colour that trembled and pulsed as the shock waves rippled through it. The feverish contagion was nothing to do with understanding the spectacle, and all to do with the giddying jolt of a thousand-volt current, charging the atmosphere and transfusing the blood. She felt strangely inside it, and yet remote, as though she saw it through the wrong end of a telescope, flattened out around a shimmering oval. Harry, on the other hand, was mentally on the pitch, his face transfigured with the strain of absolute identification – running with his teammates, turning this way and that on the ball. One moment crunched in contortions of vicarious agony, the next, appealing some corrupt decision with every ounce of his outrage, the next, exploding up in the air, crowing with exultant triumph. And, late in the second half, when the roar went up for a third goal, the stadium, already alight, blazed up into transports of delirious ecstacy that seemed to shift the whole envelope of heat-sparkle twenty feet in the air. As they rose spontaneously to their feet with the stadium, Harry grabbed hold of her and began to plant hard, furious kisses all over her hair. Indeed, would have done the same for a donkey if it had been nearby and standing reasonably still. Grown middle-aged men were kissing other totally strange middle-aged men, while the vast stadium roared and spun around them.

She was still dazed as they stumbled out, arms wrapped protectively round one another, amongst the running, milling, jubilant crowd, in danger of being trampled underfoot, towards the gate, in a tidal wave of red, white and yellow.

'Did you see him?' he bellowed. 'Did you *see* him? He's a god, Sally. Nothing short of a god. You see he's got the speed and the strength. He turns on the ball like this . . .' He began to demonstrate the move, dribbling, doubling back. 'You see, and he's so fast, they don't know what's hit 'em. Next thing . . .' He shot his foot out, scored the imaginary goal, threw his fist up in the air. 'Magic.'

The crowd bottlenecked at the exit and, as a fresh surge came up behind them, they were crushed and jostled to a standstill. 'What did you think of it?' he asked.

'I thought it was . . .' She made a visible effort to be exact. It was extraordinary, it was quite beyond words and it was dauntingly exclusive, so that whatever she said would be naive. It was like a Nürnburg rally, but she hardly thought this was the place to mention it. 'I thought it was . . . magic,' she said, and she had a look of such wide-eyes surprise that she should be saying it at all that he kissed her a friendly kiss on the side of the face, and then, because they were held there anyway, crushed by the press of the crowd, it moved round a fraction and turned into something more serious. And then the crowd moved and they pulled away.

The fans trickled down the artificial hillside like lava from a volcano. But even dispersed through the breadth of the city centre as separate streams, they filled the streets with riotous chants, climbing anything that demanded a flag or a hat, sweeping relentlessly through the squares, throwing themselves at the jetstreams of the fountains, and lolloping about, knee-deep in the water.

The sing-song, 'Liverpool, Liverpool, Liverpool . . .' seemed to echo all over the city. As they weaved through the milling fans in the Marienplatz, Sally felt a spurious sense of communion with them. It didn't make sense – she didn't share their interest, she didn't understand the game, but just having been there made a bond. They walked on, arm in arm, and she felt absurdly happy.

'And Dalglish. Could you see why they go wild for him?'

She hesitated, confessed, 'Well, I couldn't really tell one from another. They were all dressed the same . . .'

He looked at her, thunderstruck. Realising he might have to start from scratch, he took a gulp. 'Okay. Number one . . .'

'How many are there?' she asked, cautiously.

'Eleven. Now the one standing at the back, in the net, looking bored. That's the goalkeeper . . .' He was aware of her eyes becoming glassy. 'No, okay, I'm being boring.' He couldn't hope to educate her in the time allotted. 'But, you know, they've got nothing, they're nowhere, and there's just this one thing they can do, and suddenly they're up there, they're gods. *Worshipped*. It's bloody marvellous.' His face shone with satisfaction.

'Still,' said Sally, 'being worshipped probably has its problems . . .'

'Yeah, terrible problems.' He shook his head sadly. 'Money, fame, fast cars. Poor sods. Makes you want to count your blessings, doesn't it?' He made a great dumb show of locating countable blessings but fell short of his second finger. 'No, I'd be up there, mate. If it wasn't for me fallen insteps.'

'I thought it was your knees,' said Sally.

'Insteps, knees, it's all academic. I'm not there, am I?'

And he fell silent and watched the pavement, thinking uneasily about the future. As they ambled along, it seemed difficult to imagine that the thing would end, or how they would end it.

'You know I'm going to do something different when I get back,' he said suddenly. She nodded dubiously.

'Like what?' she asked.

'Oh.' He racked his brains. 'I think I'll take my life-saving certificate.' It wasn't a bad idea, now he heard it coming out of his mouth. It also sounded rather noble, unlike selling Pyrex on a market stall, which was his only other vague scheme.

'Great,' she said. 'What does that involve?'

'Oh, you know. Resuscitating dummies. Swimming in your pyjamas.'

She laughed. 'I meant what will you do with it?'

'Probably get a job as a swimming-bath attendant.' This sounded slightly less heroic. Looked at baldly, the sum reality of his lofty aspirations brought him down to earth with rather a thud. After all, it wasn't diving bronzed into the churning foam of Bondi Beach. It was counting schoolkids with a whistle.

'Well, actually,' he conceded, 'it's mostly unclogging the hair from drains.'

'Still, you probably get to save someone every now and then . . .' she said encouragingly.

'Yes. And you can do it anywhere,' he said, with an effort to recover his sense that it *did* have a certain dignity. 'I don't like to stay in the same place too long, you know? In case something turns up . . .'

For all the splendid lone-wolf ring to what he said, Sally could sense a diffidence in him, a reserve that was unfamiliar.

'Does something *always* turn up?' she asked, curiously.

He considered. 'You turned up.'

Trip to Munich, then the dates. Must be mechanically minded, German-speaking . . . he blotted it out, rather mortified. One hard-bitten middle-class feminist. The thing had pretty well swung round on him, now, he thought wryly. She had turned up and turned up with monotonous regularity and, pretty soon, he had a clear foreboding, she would turn him down.

'So, what happens now?' he asked, finally.

They came to a halt by the fountain. She watched the revelry with determined interest, trying to think what the answer was.

'I suppose you pitch the moth-eaten tent under a lamp post,' she said lightly. 'I'll hold the torch, then go back to my duck-down duvet.'

'I don't mean tonight,' he said. 'I mean after that.'

She gave a small sigh of exasperation. Why did they have to think about it now, when all it could do was bring them down to earth?

'You know what I'm saying?'

'Yes,' she said reluctantly. 'But it wouldn't work. We're different. You don't think things through.' She turned to walk away. He took her arm with more force than he meant to.

'I *have*. Thought it through. I *have*! *Right* through. I can see it quite clearly.'

'What can you see?' she asked, patiently.

Harry faltered. He closed his eyes; tried to summon up a clear projection. 'Us!'

He could get them framed in a sort of rosy vignette but the actual details refused to present themselves. She watched him curiously as he struggled with the image.

'And are we . . . smiling?' she enquired.

'Yes!' He relaxed, irritated. 'Oh, who knows, who cares? Honestly, Sally. You plan your life like it was a bullion robbery.'

It threw her off balance. Was that how he really saw her?

It conjured up such a mean, niggardly, joyless picture.

'Do I?' she asked stricken. She had no desire to be pinching and grudging in her life. She thought about it. 'Perhaps I do . . .' Because the only other answer was to follow the emotions to where they naturally led – another swirling maelstrom of muddle. And, there again, wasn't it she who was being reckless and taking chances? He was the one trying to build something solid on their flimsy base, as fast as the foundations crumbled. She said, slowly, 'I think, if that were true, I wouldn't be here, would I?'

He could see that. She had made a lot of compromises. 'No,' he said. It was best to let things flow and hope she made some more.

And as they made their way towards the beer hall, she found

herself thinking it would be quite easy just to let it carry on to some conclusion; to let the cards play out for a few more hands. It seemed almost brutal and self-destructive to turn it down. It was rare enough for anything approaching genuine warmth to come her way. If there was something masochistic in giving in to it, wasn't there something equally masochistic in denying herself some brief, intense pleasure, however ill-judged? The hall hit them with a wall of noise. The sea of diners stretched back so far it just became a muzzy haze in the smoke-filled atmosphere. Above the high babble of voices, an oompah band ground out remorselessly jolly tunes, and whenever a melody finished tables of Bavarian men with square mountain faces swayed in maudlin unison and took up the refrain. At the far end of the hall, behind the musicians, the stage was set with an elaborate painted backdrop and large painted pines to mimic a grotto. Across this expanse of kitsch, a stout pine log was resting on two stakes, for what reason Sally couldn't guess. Underneath it there appeared to be a large deep tub. The waitresses, glistening with exertion, were propelled this way and that by the sheer weight of the giant beer glasses they carried, sometimes twelve to a fist, and they crisscrossed each other towards the dark oak tables with extraordinary adroitness and strength.

Two beers slammed down on the table in front of them. It was all Sally could do to lift the great glass to her lips. Dotted about the room were rogue patches of red and the chants occasionally filtered through as a thin wail.

Harry was doing some rapid thinking. People could change. They did change. Just because his life so far was like snakes and ladders, it didn't preclude some radical reshuffle – it might take time, but it was possible. The Eros Hotel, of course, would have to go. He could not see Sally sitting primly on his truckle bed, examining the quality of his horse blanket, entertained by the too intimate gurglings of another inmate's plumbing. His little boxroom cost sixty pounds a week, and his average earnings when he was in casual work were ninety. It was no place to conduct a romance.

The picture flared up too vividly in his mind and he pushed it down. His fresh start had to involve a fairly well-paid job with enough spare cash to get a one-bedroom flat. He chose to forget the dispiriting six-month search around the newsagents' windows across rain-smelling pavements. He put aside the fact that London flats changed by word of mouth among the middle classes. The postcards on the board were for hard-up foreigners and people who didn't know anyone, and they usually led to high-ceilinged hallways with mould bubbling the forties wallpaper off rotten plaster, multi-occupation firetraps or pretend hotels.

'I thought I might look for a flat when I get back,' he said casually.

'It's tricky in London right now,' she said. It occurred to her that Laurie was well in with a housing association and might be able to pull a few strings. Then she pulled herself up sharply. This was to assume she would see him again. Part of her was being swept along with his assumptions. But what was he assuming, she asked herself.

Harry ticked it off. A flat, a steady job and a life that followed a rather calmer pattern, without the peaks and troughs that gave his present life the fevered oscillations of a seismograph needle.

He had a hazy idea that it was easier to lock into an amorphous middle stratum. Normal jobs, the kind he could get, needed a grinding commitment that was rewarded neither with advancement nor financial gain. But there was some classless band in the middle – social workers, journalists, market researchers – freelance people.

He had a vague idea you got into social work through community service, and community service through petty crime.

'Do you think I could be a journalist?' he asked her suddenly.

Some curious ritual was being enacted on the podium. His question penetrated her awareness just as a fanfare went up from the band, sending a ripple of anticipation through the crowd.

'It's only a matter of having opinions,' he was saying. 'I've got opinions, it's just no one wants to hear them.'

Members of the audience were surging up towards the stage, tripping over one another in their rush. The M.C. kept up a constant running patter, goading them with sly insinuation; the audience responded and rocked the room with good-natured uproar. Two beefy Bavarians were let through from the mass, were clambering up on to the greasy pole, gripping it with mountain thighs as each took hold of a solid, sausage-shaped bolster and began to whack and flail at each other with determined glee. They swayed this way and that under the blows, wobbling dangerously with the sideways momentum, swiping wildly in the air.

'I'm sure you could do anything you set your mind to . . .' she said absently, her eyes on the bizarre show.

Large fat men with multiple chins and droll, rolling eyes were mopping their streaming tears, shaking like great blancmanges, endangering their monstrous steins of foaming beer.

He probably *could* do anything he set his mind to, she thought, given the right break. He was emphatically ruled out of garage jobs or camping shops, but those apart, he had intelligence, dogged persistence and he was undeniably good with people.

Contestants were following thick and fast upon the heels of others as they thwacked and threshed and tumbled into the water tank below. The crowd erupted in hysteria. Grown men jostled up the front, heaving and pushing for the ignominy of being bonked and laughed at, and plunged into a tub of water. Sally was at a loss to understand it. As one fell off, the other swung wildly under, trying to keep his grip, hanging on like grim death.

'I mean, most people seem to have a structure to their lives . . .' he persisted earnestly. He seemed to be saying something important to her but the laughter and the whooping drowned his words. He saw she was distracted, broke concentration to follow her gaze.

'Pathetic, isn't it?' he said. Gross, overweight men whacking each other with pretend sausages. There was an uncompromising vulgarity about it that reminded him of *It's a Knockout* or Butlin's. People were quite unselfconscious. They entered into the ribald

163

spirit with total abandon. He watched them as they bobbed and ducked and thumped, and thought that, once, not so long ago, in fact about last week, this would have held a certain appeal, but now it seemed part of something far off and distant. His eyes dimly focused on the scrolled motto above the stage: PREIS 800 DM. He supposed that meant there'd been some earlier event at eight o'clock.

'Yes,' she said, as two more contestants hauled themselves up, helpless with laughter, shaking off the water. 'The things people do for money.'

'So what I'm trying to say,' he struggled on. Then her words filtered through. His eyes shot up to the scroll. Eight hundred deutschmarks. He tried to keep his voice casual.

'Er . . . Sally, out of interest, how much is that on the exchange?'

'About two hundred pounds,' she answered automatically. Before she could blink her eyes, he was on his feet, pulling off his shirt, rubbing and spitting on his hands, striding out through the crowd towards the podium. He disappeared into the scrum, pushing and shoving, asserting his rights.

She got to her feet and watched dismayed as he emerged on the stage, seeing off the competition, then clambering eagerly on to the greasy pole and taking up his bolster like a lance. He began to biff at his opponent and the man flailed back and nearly knocked him off in one. Their arms were swinging like sails and the blows were quite a serious weight.

She was frozen with intense embarrassment. It went through her like a chill from childhood when an accompanying adult decided to have an argument in a shop. A shrinking horror of making oneself conspicuous, an apprehension of impending mortifying doom. Surely nothing was worth the indignity of plunging into water, hoarse and spluttering, to hoots of derision from the crowd. But Harry was holding his own, feinting this way and that, teasing his opponent, then moving in and thumping straight-on blows until the man dodged too far and swung around the pole, pulled off by the next eager replacement. Harry shuffled along the pole, excitedly, getting a better grip with his thighs. The other man lunged and rained hefty whacks at his head. Sally winced, feeling every blow for him, willing him to avoid the inevitable ducking that would reduce him, somehow, to the scale he really was. Harry let the hail of blows find their mark, with soft, stunning thuds. She wondered why he didn't swerve or duck. And then, she realised, as he came back at his attacker, that it was part of a technique. It whipped the opponent up to wilder and more frenzied swipes, describing bigger arcs until the aggressor's balance teetered and then Harry darted in and boffed at him, head-on, bringing the bolster down again and again, in decisive slams, until the other lost his precarious perch and it was taken up by whoever had fought through the clamour to try his luck. He brought down four or five this way, and now they were coming at him thick and fast, each more aggressive than the last, grimacing and grinding their teeth in mock menace, lashing with over-enthusiastic swings, each following the last one's fate. Harry sat triumphant, sweating with exertion, his eyes dancing waiting for the next. The crowd was alive now. The supporters recognised their own and were on their feet to him. And, as yet another mountainous hulk fell away, Harry began to relax and enjoy himself and let his natural showmanship take over. The noise roared in his ears; the Liverpool boys began to chant, 'Eas-ee. Eas-ee'. Harry turned to acknowledge the adulation, arms high in the air like a conquering hero, exulting in his body. The sea of faces swarmed before him and the cheers rang like a buzz in his ears, as if he were back in the stadium, but they were all for him.

Sally relaxed. The ridiculous spectacle was ennobled now, its essence distilled to some higher abstraction. It didn't matter that his achievement was only hanging on to a greasy pole, fighting grown men off with floppy bolsters, the essence was the same as if he'd scored a goal, or fought a Spanish bull or ridden the unridable horse in some cliché-ridden western, it was the same peak of physicality, the same male celebration. Harry was King, and he was entitled to wring every ounce from it. While he exulted to the crowd, a youth slipped on beside him and struck him a crafty sideways swipe that nearly stunned him. She gasped. He teetered, almost fell, and just pulled back in time to rally and labour blows on his tormentor's head. The MC started to count, as though knocking something down at auction; at last a claxon rang, and he announced it over. He handed Harry down and, thrusting the fan of deutschmarks into his hand, paraded him about the stage. She watched it all, remote, half-smiling. He punched the air with his spread of notes, turning this way and that to the crowd's uproar. She felt an odd qualm of inadequacy, as though he were a different breed of animal she couldn't hope to understand, feeling like an anxious, housebound Wendy watching Peter Pan fly round the curtains.

And as he came to leave the stage, he suddenly remembered Sally, and a flicker of anxiety crossed his eyes. Whatever picture he'd been building for her, he knew he'd blown it. He scanned the crowd, across the jubilant supporters. Maybe she'd stalked off in disgust. Then he located her, standing alone in a shadow by the curtain. Their eyes met. She smiled. He thought it was all right.

Chapter 14

He woke around four. He tried to get back to sleep but there were too many things buzzing round his brain. He lit a cigarette and watched it glimmer in the half light, watched the smoke unfurling, and when he bored of that, he watched the green radium digits slotting over on the large electronic clock. He thought what doors the money opened. Two hundred pounds. They could have a good time on it. They could eke it out maybe and see some more of Germany. He saw them in his mind's eye on a train. His powers of visualisation were always stronger at night, and much stronger when the co-star of his fantasy was safely asleep in one of her own and couldn't block his transmissions. The train was like a Hornby Dublo, passing through a scenic layout of rounded hillocks, the grass like green felt on a vacuum-formed moulding. They were opening sandwiches, trying halting German out on fellow passengers. He switched tack. He wasn't very good at eking out money. Or they could blow it – a good restaurant, obsequious waiters, champagne. He saw himself in a suit. He wished he'd had the forethought to bring it with him, the one he'd borrowed for the meeting in the ICA. Well, perhaps he could get a suit cheap, try not to dig too deep into the beano money. He dragged on his cigarette. None of it quite cut ice. What was blocking it, he knew, was the solid sheaf of paper in a plastic spine just beside the clock. He didn't know what the women's stuff meant but he was quite alert to its threat. There was something about the solidity of the soft-bound book that was depressing. It represented a body of opinions, and judging by the thickness she had quite a lot of those. The question was, which was the real Sally? The one that stared austerely from the bedside table, no doubt entirely serious and reasoned, or the flesh and blood one, sleeping with her mouth half-open and her arm across his chest?

He became aware of a soft, electronic purring in the room. It was the phone discreetly buzzing with an insistent red light. He wondered who could be calling at four in the morning.

'Hallo?' he whispered.

'Hallo?' It was a cautious woman's voice. *'Kann ich spreche zu Fraulein Francis?'* The German was halting and the accent unmistakably East End.

He looked down at Sally. The sprinkling of orange freckles across the dead white of her shoulder. The street lights made pale stripes across the bedclothes.

'Look, I think you've got the wrong number,' he said. 'It's the middle of the night.'

'I'm trying to reach my friend, Fraulein Francis. They said they'd put me through and I've got you, are you the desk?'

He thought about it. If this was a close friend, would Sally want to be compromised by him passing her over? Whoever it was, he thought it could wait till morning. He adopted what he fondly imagined to be a German accent with an American twang.

'Yes, I am the desk,' he purred. 'We do not usually put calls through at this time of night.'

'Well, will you give her a message, then?' said the voice. 'Tell her it's Kay, and I'm in Munich . . .'

'Hold on, I'll just get that down . . .' said Harry, making a rustle that might have been writing but wasn't.

Kay waited patiently. She was standing in a booth in the Hauptbahnhof. The station was quite lively for the time of night, if one counted the contents of the sleeping bags, laid out like rows of sausages in batter, and the policemen strolling in pairs, passing time till the dawn. She was running on adrenalin. With the suddenness of her flight and the momentous nature of the decision she had taken, she felt the need to communicate it to someone, anyone.

'Tell her, she was right. You can't think one thing and do something else, and I'm in Munich . . .' She waited for him to jot that down.

Harry pulled up with a jolt. 'Here, hold on,' he said. 'Why can't you? Excuse me for butting in but I'd say that was the whole beauty of the human brain. It's capable of handling lots of different conflicting concepts at once.'

Kay looked at the receiver, disconcerted. She wanted to leave a message, not to continue the wearisome debate that had racketed off the walls of the little council flat for the last week.

'Your English is very good,' she said.

He recollected himself. 'Er . . . my Mother was English. I spent many happy times in your country.' On both counts this was true. He eased himself back into the role.

Kay had a surreal sensation that the German had slipped in and out of a Liverpudlian phase, but she was tired and thought it was probably her ears playing tricks. But it put her in mind of something else. Hadn't *he* been from Liverpool? Sally's Good Deed? She resolved to try asking the desk man something confidential. She lowered her voice, delicately.

'Look, I hope you don't mind my asking . . . but, you know the English girl? Is she on her own?'

'Yes.'

'There isn't anyone odd hanging round her?'

'No!' said Harry, stung.

Kay smiled, relieved. 'Well, thanks for all your help. And if you could just tell her I'll see her tomorrow.'

The line clicked and turned into a non-committal buzz. Harry stared dully at the receiver, took the last hard draw on his fag and stubbed it out. Well, he thought, trying to muster some grim comfort from it all, it meant he didn't have to buy the suit. He could see it clearly now, from a distance, as someone else might see it, looking on. He didn't belong any more. And how would Sally explain him to her friend? If two thoughts couldn't be supported, where was he? Someone odd hanging around her.

He heard Sally saying with that strained note he had heard in the schloss, 'Er . . . this is my friend, Harry . . .' and then he tried to drown out the priggish tone he had given to her voice. He knew it wasn't a fair picture. After all, she was there beside him. That wasn't a figment of his imagination.

He supposed it was up to him to do what had to be done. He levered himself gently from the bed and went over to his clothes. He hummed very softly as he pulled his jeans on. Whether he hummed for company or in the hope she would stir and say, 'Where are you going?' he didn't know.

He walked around the bed, stiffly so that his jacket wouldn't creak, took out his billfold from his pocket. Two hundred pounds. It was hers really. For the petrol, for the parts, for the gaol bond, for the rockery. It all added up. He pulled over the hotel notepad and scribbled a quick note. Then tore the page very gently from the gum that sealed it. He moved towards the door, then hesitated. He *had* paid for a few things. There was such a thing as taking a noble gesture too far. He turned back and took fifty deutschmarks from the pile. He looked at her, sprawled innocent in sleep, then closed the door behind him.

And, as he walked out along the lonely, early morning street in the blue light of dawn, he relived his heroic moment, remembered the crowd noise ringing in his ears. He set his face like granite and strode out, a solitary figure dwarfed by the high apartment blocks to either side, and the refrain he had been humming persisted in his head, until it swelled up with the sad, sweet twang of Frankie Laine's voice. 'Do not forsake me, oh my darlin', On this our weddin' day-ee, Do not forsake me, Oh my darlin', wait along . . . I do not know what fate awaits me . . . I only know I must be brave . . . for I must face the man who hates me . . . or lie a coward . . . or lie a coward . . .' He swung his bag up on his shoulder and walked on out to where the coaches were.

The football fans were massing in the square just as dawn was breaking imperceptibly through the haze. The air was cold. The fountain spray slapped the pavement and gave off a smell of damp concrete. As he moved amongst them, a couple recognised him from the night before, hailed him like a long-lost friend, drew him into their midst. He felt his spirits lifting. This was his setting, not the other. He began to negotiate for a lift, and as they rallied round and tried to sort him out, he felt a great warmth towards them and a great sense of bond. These were his mates; people who had it written in their faces, in their voices that they came out of the same beginnings, shared a common lot. All contemplating work tomorrow, or finding work tomorrow, but for now blocking out the next set of problems in the hope of extending the holiday past its limits by sheer willpower.

As the coach pulled out, they started up their repertoire of songs and passed around a crate of beer.

Kay was pacing the hotel room, retelling what had passed – Keith's insistence that she drop the job and become a real housewife like all the other mothers in the block. He was adamant that this was the answer to their problems. If it was the job that made the house and child a shared responsibility, then nothing was simpler. She should just jack in the job.

'I could see what he was doing,' Kay was saying. 'Get me locked up in that little box. I mean the job's not much but at least it gets me out. I don't know what he wants. I said to him, it's all making allowances, giving in. It's not give and take, it's all one-sided . . . I said to him, you married me 'cos I was lively and . . . interesting and now you want to turn me into some sort of cabbage . . .' She stopped suddenly. ''Ere, are you listening to me?' Sally was sitting on the bed, lost in her own thoughts.

Sally looked up, shook her head. 'Sorry.'

'I could have stayed at home and not been listened to,' said Kay, a touch peeved. Her eyes fell upon the letter, she picked it up. She began to read it out with increasing mystification.

'This thing is bigger than both of us. I'm gonna make it easy on you. I'm hitting the trail. Use the money to bring the kid up decent . . .' She looked up, alarmed. 'What kid?'

Sally smiled reluctantly to herself. She had a curious, wan, empty feeling. The feeling that it *might* have been possible. That the differences which separated them *might* have been superable.

Kay saw the smile. 'I reckon it's just as well I came when I did,' she said. She waited for Sally to say something in explanation but nothing was forthcoming.

'This is nice,' said Kay, holding up the musical box. She

171

pressed the lever and it began to tinkle. She watched it with simple fascination. 'Not your sort of thing though.'

As they walked through the door of the conference centre, Sally was aware of an odd sense of fragmentation. The women were a broad cross-section of age, type and nationality, and there were a lot of them. Seen as a mass, their bright clothes made a crazy collage of texture and pattern. The noise level was high but qualitatively different from the kind of noise a mass of men could make. It was too much of a shift of perspective to make so abruptly – as though the world had tilted violently one way on its axis and was now tilting back with equal force. She became aware of someone plucking nervously at her elbow and realised that Kay was intimidated by their confidence, their seriousness and their flamboyance. She rallied and, taking Kay's arm, pushed through to the registration desk.

There were maybe two hundred women in the seminar, and as the morning moved on, and the pair of them relaxed, Sally found herself taken aback by the extraordinary energy in the room. It was out of all proportion to the numbers, and she could see the startling disparity all the more clearly for seeing it with Kay's fresh, unaccustomed eyes. As speaker succeeded speaker with careful, impassioned speeches, she felt a great surge of exhilaration. It wasn't as though she hadn't been in situations of extraordinary voltage in the last few days, but this was quite different. It came out of serious confident thought and was directed towards specific goals for change. Kay felt the same thing too – a sense of worms turning quietly in the subsoil. And the thoughts Sally spared for Harry were to do with wishing she'd had a little longer to make him understand that what he thought of as irrelevant was anything but. Then she smiled wryly to herself. Actually, she wished she could have had a little longer with him, full stop. In fact it was unlikely they would have talked about politics.

Out on the autobahn, the football coaches sped along, festooned with the flags and banners, ringing with the supporters' voices as they gave full throat to their repertoire of ditties. There was a kind of desperate *joie de vivre* in the pulling of the beer cans, and the lugging out of crates. Germany was slipping away, most of them had to go to work tomorrow and no one wanted the holiday to end. Harry was in good spirits. He was aware that the speeding fields brought him closer to reality, but he didn't mind reality too much, because it was where he normally had to live. He was planning to have a hamburger when he got to London. He hadn't been allowed one since the sausage incident. The songs were becoming filthier and filthier and Harry prevailed upon them to change the tune. He started them up on 'Do not forsake me oh my darling', partly for sentimental reasons, and partly because, against all the other tunes that had been rising from the bus, it still unaccountably kept going round and round in his head.

DELIVERANCE

JAMES DICKEY

Four men set out from a small Southern town for a three-day camping and canoe trip . . . a holiday jaunt that turns into a nightmare struggle for survival.

This is much more than a terrifying story of violence – murderous violence, sexual violence, and the violence of nature – it is a brilliant study of human beings driven towards – and sometimes beyond – the limits of endurance.

Shattering, spellbinding, and a masterly piece of writing, *Deliverance* has been described as the classic novel of male conflict and survival.

'A novel that will curl your toes . . . the limit of dramatic tension'
New York Times

'A brilliant tale of action'
Observer

'A fast, shapely adventure tale'
Time Magazine

'Brilliant and breathtaking'
New Yorker

0 349 10076 4
ABACUS FICTION

BETTY BLUE

PHILIPPE DJIAN

The major European best seller that was made into the celebrated film.

'A brilliant, painful account of a doomed love affair. While the storm clouds are gathering, the teller of the story believes the picnic is forever. Much, much better than the film'
Carlo Gébler

'A powerful, picaresque tale of a relationship which moves into the frenetic and finally the tragic'
Yorkshire Post

'A simple story of love found and thwarted that also becomes a remarkable journey backward: from modernist narrative resignation and ennui into full-fledged emotional engagement, complication, deepening of character and resolution . . . The transformation of character is powerful, convincing, reverberant; the love story is sad and fine'
Kirkus Reviews

'Djian is a major writer. A page of his prose reads like nothing else, except perhaps another page of his. His writing is the real thing'
Le Monde

'An atmosphere reminiscent of, by turns, *Diva* and *Paris, Texas* . . . Djian's books soar above those of his contemporaries'
Paris Match

0 349 10110 8
ABACUS FICTION

Abacus now offers an exciting range of quality fiction and non-fiction by both established and new authors. All of the books in this series are available from good bookshops, or can be ordered from the following address:

Sphere Books
Cash Sales Department
P.O. Box 11
Falmouth
Cornwall, TR10 9EN.

Please send cheque or postal order (no currency), and allow 60p for postage and packing for the first book plus 25p for the second book and 15p for each additional book ordered up to a maximum charge of £1.90 in U.K.

B.F.P.O. customers please allow 60p for the first book, 25p for the second book plus 15p per copy for the next 7 books, thereafter 9p per book.

Overseas customers, including Eire, please allow £1.25 for postage and packing for the first book, 75p for the second book and 28p for each subsequent title ordered.